WHISPER

Cerberus Personal Security Specialists
Book 3

ELLIE MASTERS
MASTER OF ROMANTIC SUSPENSE

JEM Publishing

This book is dedicated to my one and only—my amazing and wonderful husband.

Without your care and support, my writing would not have made it this far.

You pushed me when I needed to be pushed.

You supported me when I felt discouraged.

You believed in me when I didn't believe in myself.

If it weren't for you, this book never would have come to life.

SUGGESTED READING ORDER

START HERE

Rockstar Romance

The Angel Fire Rock Romance Series

EACH BOOK IN THIS SERIES CAN BE READ AS A STANDALONE AND IS ABOUT A DIFFERENT COUPLE WITH AN **HEA**.

IT IS RECOMMENDED THEY ARE READ IN ORDER.

Heart's Insanity

Ashes to New

Heart's Desire

Heart's Collide

Hearts Divided

Hearts Entwined

Forest's FALL

Hearts The Last Beat

CONTINUE HERE…

Military Romance

Guardian Hostage Rescue Specialists

Rescuing Melissa

(Get a FREE copy of Rescuing Melissa when you join Ellie's Newsletter)

Alpha Team

Rescuing Zoe

Rescuing Moira

Rescuing Eve

Rescuing Lily

Rescuing Jinx

Rescuing Maria

Bravo Team

Rescuing Angie

Rescuing Isabelle

Rescuing Carmen

Rescuing Rosalie

Rescuing Kaye

Cara's Protector

Rescuing Barbi

Charlie Team

Rescuing Rebel

Rescuing Stitch

Rescuing Mia

Jenna's Protector

Rescuing Sophia

Rescuing Malia

Rescuing Ally (Part 1)

Rescuing Ally (Part 2)

Delta Team

Rescuing Ember

Rescuing Aria

*STANDALONES IN THE GUARDIAN HOSTAGE RESCUE
SERIES YOU CAN READ ANYTIME*

Military Romance

Guardian Personal Protection Specialists

Sybil's Protector

Lyra's Protector

Angel's Peak Series

Steamy Instalove Small Town

EACH BOOK IN THIS SERIES CAN BE READ AS A STANDALONE AND IS ABOUT A DIFFERENT COUPLE WITH AN HEA.

Snowed in with the Mountain Doctor

Rescued by the Mountain Guide

Stranded with the Resort Owner

Matched with the Small-Town Chef

Trapped with the Forest Ranger

Snowbound with the Vineyard Owner

Reunited with the Hometown Hero

Colliding with the Coffee Shop Owner

Falling for the Firefighter

Wrecked with the Reclusive Author

Tangled with the Single Dad

Whirlwinded by the Helicopter Pilot

Sheltered by the Veterinarian

Bound by the Sheriff

The One I Want Series

(Small Town, Military Heroes)

By Jet & Ellie Masters

Ellie Masters writing as L.A. Warren

Vendel Rising: a Science Fiction Serialized Novel

If you enjoyed this book by Ellie Masters, the LIGHTER SIDE of the Jet & Ellie writing duo, and aren't afraid of edgier writing, you might enjoy reading BDSM themed books written by Jet, the DARKER SIDE of the Masters' Writing Team.

The DARKER SIDE

Jet Masters is the darker side of the Jet & Ellie writing duo!

Romantic Suspense

Changing Roles Series:

THIS SERIES MUST BE READ IN ORDER.

Command Me

Control Me

Collar Me

Embracing FATE

Seizing FATE

Accepting FATE

HOT READS

A STANDALONE NOVEL.

Down the Rabbit Hole

Light BDSM Romance

The Ties that Bind

To My Readers

This book is a work of fiction. It does not exist in the real world and should not be construed as reality. As in most romantic fiction, I've taken liberties. I've compressed the romance into a sliver of time. I've allowed these characters to develop strong bonds of trust over a matter of days.

This does not happen in real life where you, my amazing readers, live. Take more time in your romance and learn who you're giving a piece of your heart to. I urge you to move with caution. Always protect yourself.

Grab the First Book in The Guardian Hostage Rescue Specialists Series for Free

https://elliemasters.com/RescuingMelissa

ONE

Eliza

PATTERNS IN THE NOISE

Three of my colleagues are dead, and I just figured out why someone murdered them.

The pattern on my computer screen shouldn't exist. Roman military ciphers from 47 BC shouldn't share mathematical frequencies with modern encryption protocols. The correlation is too precise for coincidence—actually, the probability of coincidence is 0.000034%, which rounds to impossible in any practical application.

"This can't be right," I tell the empty office, because talking through problems helps me think, even when no one's listening. "Unless someone's using historical analysis as a cover for— Oh. Oh no."

The fluorescent lights hum above me, that steady electrical buzz most people find annoying, but has become my companion. It's consistent. Predictable. Unlike the data glowing on my three monitors, which refuses to make sense.

My office in Georgetown's Healy Hall feels like a medieval tower tonight—stone walls, Gothic windows, shadows that seem to move when I'm not looking directly at them. The building impresses visitors during daylight, but at night, with most windows dark, it transforms into something from a horror story.

My fingers fly across the keyboard, pulling up recent papers from my collaborative research group. Professor Sarah Williams at Yale, researching Byzantine cryptography. Dr. David Kim at MIT, analyzing medieval cipher patterns. Dr. Lisa Parker at Stanford, studying Renaissance encryption methods.

All of us funded by the same grant. All of us finding similar anomalies in our respective historical periods.

The phone buzzes. My sister's text from Portland: **Still at the office? Get a life, El.**

Quick fingers tap back: **Have a life. It involves fascinating dead Romans.**

Her response arrives instantly: **Dead being the operative word. When's the last time you went on a date?**

The phone returns to its spot beside scattered research notes because we both know the answer. Eight months since Dr. Stefan Whitfield from the History Department—brilliant on paper, accomplished in reality, passionate about ancient civilizations—right up until he announced that my "verbal processing" exhausted him and suggested I learn to "enjoy comfortable silence."

Before Stefan, there was James, the investigative journalist who initially found my expertise captivating until he discovered that my analysis extends to everything, including relationships. And before James, there was Thomas, the software engineer who appreciated my intelligence but couldn't tolerate what he termed my "need to narrate every thought."

The pattern repeats itself: initial attraction, growing irritation, eventual abandonment. Men drawn to intelligence who flee from its verbal expression. Academic types with weak handshakes and tentative kisses that felt more like research than passion.

None of them sparked anything beyond intellectual curiosity. When physical intimacy became awkward fumbling between sheets, ending the relationships felt more like relief than loss.

Not that my fantasy life suffers from such limitations. Late nights studying Roman military campaigns have produced far more interesting companions than Georgetown's academic dating pool.

A gladiator wouldn't ask permission before claiming what he wanted. No hesitant touches or apologetic fumbling—just powerful hands pinning me against stone walls, demanding submission with actions rather than words. Bronze skin gleaming with arena sweat, muscles earned through combat rather than university gyms. He'd drop me to my knees without explanation, take what pleased him, make me beg for more with guttural sounds instead of words.

Heat floods my cheeks as the fantasy dissolves back into fluorescent-lit reality. Apparently, two thousand years of civilization haven't improved on certain masculine qualities. Give me a warrior over a weakling any day.

Too bad modern men seem threatened by women who use their voices. Stefan actually suggested meditation to "learn the beauty of silence." James recommended I "listen more, talk less" to improve our relationship dynamic. Thomas bought me a journal, claiming I could "process thoughts privately instead of constantly verbalizing."

All three missed the fundamental point: verbal processing defines who I am. Fighting it would be like holding my breath until unconsciousness. Not that it mattered—they were all too weak to force me to do either.

Now, a Roman gladiator—he wouldn't waste time with suggestions. He'd be strong enough to shut me up, kissing me senseless until words became impossible, or putting my mouth to far better uses than talking. Heat spirals through my core at the thought of being rendered speechless by pleasure instead of politeness.

Get a grip, Eliza. Roman gladiators are two thousand years dead, and fantasies about impossible men don't solve real problems.

My focus returns to the puzzle. "So if this frequency distribution matches modern patterns, then either the Romans achieved sophistication we've never suspected, or—"

The computer completes its analysis, and words die in my throat.

Embedded within what should be two-thousand-year-old Roman military dispatches, my pattern recognition software—created during my DoD years—has detected modern encryption. Not similar to modern. Actually modern. Created within the last year.

"What the hell?"

This is exactly what Sarah found three weeks ago. She called at midnight, excited and confused. "Eliza, you need to see this. I'm finding modern crypto signatures in Byzantine texts. That's impossible, right?"

David confirmed it a week later. His mathematical analysis showed contemporary encryption algorithms hidden within historical documents from our shared research database. "It's like someone is using ancient texts as camouflage for modern communications," he said during our last video call. "But who would do that? And why hide it in our research?"

Lisa was last, just ten days ago. Her linguistic analysis revealed that someone was actively using our research project as a cover for encrypted communications. "We need to be careful," she warned in her final email. "This feels like something we weren't supposed to find."

Now I'm staring at the same discovery. Modern encryption hidden in ancient texts. Someone is using our academic research as a pipeline for coded messages.

"Oh shit. Oh shit, shit, shit."

My blood chills—actually, that's not accurate. Blood doesn't change temperature from fear. The sympathetic nervous system triggers vasoconstriction, reducing blood flow to the extremities, which creates the sensation of coldness while maintaining core temperature. I'm babbling in my own head—that's never good.

I pull up our shared research folder. Sarah's last login: fifteen days ago. David's: nine days ago. Lisa's: five days ago.

I shouldn't pull up the news reports, but I can't stop myself. It still doesn't feel real.

Stanford Professor Dies in Apparent Suicide.

The article is from two days ago. She jumped from her apartment building. Survived by her husband and two daughters. Eight and ten years old. Lisa showed me pictures at the last conference, talked about their college funds, their piano lessons, their—

MIT Researcher Dies in Car Accident.

The article is dated five days ago. Dr. David Kim, 34, a brilliant mathematician who could calculate probabilities faster than most computers. His car went off a bridge. No skid marks.

My hands shake as I pull up Sarah's name.

Yale Professor Dies in Apartment Fire.

Yesterday. Oh God, yesterday. While I was sitting here playing with patterns, Sarah was burning to death in a fire that started from "faulty wiring" in a building that was renovated last year.

The pattern in my data isn't historical. It's current. Active. Someone is using our academic research as cover for modern communications, and everyone who discovers it dies in a different type of accident.

Three accidents. Three different methods. Statistical probability of three researchers in the same collaborative group dying within a week? I don't need to calculate it. It's murder. Murder disguised as accidents, which means whoever's doing this has resources, planning, and the ability to make deaths look natural.

My secure phone—the one from my DoD days—sits in my desk drawer. Dr. James Morrison, my former handler when I did encryption work for the Defense Department. He's FBI now—wouldn't give details about what division—but said to call if I ever stumbled onto something dangerous.

Three dead colleagues qualify as dangerous.

"Morrison." His voice sounds tired, like it always does.

"James, it's Eliza Wren. I need— God, I don't even know how to explain this. Do you know about the linguistic pattern analysis grant I'm working on?"

"The historical cipher project, right? What about it?"

"Three of my co-researchers are dead. All within the last week. Different types of accidents, but James, I found something in the data. Modern encryption hidden in historical frameworks. Someone's using our research as cover for current communications, and everyone who finds it…" My voice cracks. Sarah had a cat named Schrödinger. She made physics jokes about him being simultaneously fed and unfed until observed.

"Where are you right now?"

"My office. Georgetown. Healy Hall, third floor."

"Pack everything related to this research. Hard drives, papers, everything. Then get out. Do you have somewhere safe to go?"

"My apartment? It's just a few blocks—"

"No. Somewhere unexpected. Somewhere you've never mentioned at work." A pause, heavy with meaning. "If what you're saying is true, they're probably already watching you."

They. Not *someone*. They.

"James, who are *they*?"

"I don't know, but three dead academics aren't a coincidence. Pack your research, leave campus, but stay public. Crowds. Witnesses. Don't go anywhere isolated."

"Should I call the police?"

"No. If this is what I think it might be, local law enforcement can't help. Just get your research and get out. Drive normally, don't run, don't act suspicious. Just a professor heading home after a late night."

The call ends. My hands shake as I grab backup drives—three of them, because redundancy in data storage is essential. Pattern recognition algorithms, frequency analyses, and six months of work that apparently decoded something deadly.

I stuff everything into my messenger bag, then think better of it. The go-bag in my filing cabinet—paranoid habit from my DoD days—makes more sense. Change of clothes, cash, basic supplies. I transfer the drives, adding my laptop and printed papers I can't leave behind.

The building feels different now. Every shadow could hide someone. Every footstep in the hallway makes my heart rate spike—approximately 120 bpm if my carotid pulse is accurate. Fight or flight response, completely normal given the circumstances, but knowing the physiological mechanism doesn't make it stop.

I lock my office and walk down the hallway like it's any other night. The Gothic architecture that once felt romantic now feels oppressive. Stone walls, designed to last centuries, couldn't protect Sarah, David, or Lisa.

Outside, campus life continues normally—students walking between dorms, laughter on the crisp October air. Everything proceeds as if the world hasn't shifted beneath my feet.

A dark van sits across the street. I noticed it on Tuesday and assumed it was for construction or maintenance. The van hasn't moved in three days.

"You're paranoid, Eliza. It's just a van." But my voice shakes.

I head off campus, hands steady despite the adrenaline surge. Pedestrian and automobile traffic shows nothing unusual. Just normal D.C. traffic. The city never sleeps, which works in my favor. Witnesses. Crowds. Safety in numbers.

Except I need to go back.

The realization hits at a red light. The physical drives have data, but the algorithm itself—the key to understanding what I found—is only on my office computer. I encrypted it, password-protected it, but didn't copy it because it was still running. Still processing. Still finding patterns that shouldn't exist.

Without that algorithm, the data is just noise. With it, I can prove what these communications are, maybe decode them fully.

"This is stupid," I tell myself, already turning around. "Horror movie victim levels of stupid. The etymology of 'stupid' comes from Latin "stupere," meaning stunned or amazed, which is exactly what I'll be when someone kills me for going back. But I need that algorithm."

Campus is quiet at night. The lights at Healy Hall are mostly off except for security lighting and a few graduate student offices. Normal. Everything looks normal.

My key card beeps softly at the side door. The elevator feels too confined, too vulnerable, so I take the stairs. Three flights, footsteps echoing despite my attempts to be quiet.

The hallway is dark except for emergency lighting. My office door is exactly as I left it—locked, undisturbed. The algorithm is still running on my computer, still finding patterns someone's willing to kill to keep hidden. I take a seat, entranced, eager to solve this puzzle, and that's how I lose track of time. Before I know it, it's way past midnight, and I'm exactly where Morrison told me not to be.

I save everything to a flash drive, then delete it from the system. Scorched earth approach—if they come looking, they'll find nothing. The drive goes into my bra because it's the safest place.

Paranoid? Maybe. But three colleagues thought they were safe too.

A sound in the hallway freezes me. Footsteps. Multiple sets. Moving with purpose, not the wandering gait of students or the hurried pace of a late professor.

They're here.

My office has one door, three windows, and no other exit. Windows face a three-story drop onto concrete. The door leads to a hallway now containing multiple approaching footsteps.

I grab my go-bag and do the only thing I can think of—hide under my desk like this is an earthquake drill, like ducking and covering will save me from professional killers.

My phone vibrates. Morrison.

"James," I whisper. "They're here. In my building. Multiple footsteps."

"You're still at work? Jesus, Eliza, get out. Now."

"I can't. They're in the hallway. Third floor, nowhere to—"

"Someone is on the way."

"Who?"

"A friend from Cerberus. Hide. Stay quiet. He'll be there soon."

"Who? How soon? James—"

"Just hide. Help is coming."

The footsteps stop outside my door. The handle turns slowly, testing, finding it locked.

Then silence.

Silence is worse than noise. Silence means they're thinking, planning, preparing. The etymology of 'silence' comes from Latin "silere," meaning to be still, but there's nothing still about this moment. This is active silence, predatory silence, the pause before—

Something clicks in the lock. Soft. Professional.

They're coming in.

I pull my knees to my chest, making myself as small as possible under the desk. Go-bag pressed against my ribs. Flash drive cutting into skin beneath my bra. Heart hammering so loud they must hear it.

The door opens with a creak in the hinges I've been meaning to oil for months.

A footstep. Another. Careful. Searching.

I hold my breath, close my eyes, and wait for help that probably won't come in time.

Sarah. David. Lisa.

I'm about to become the fourth accident.

Unless Morrison's help is very, very close.

TWO

Cooper

SILENT RUNNING

F‍OUR HOURS OF PERFECT SILENCE.

The Seattle waterfront spreads below my position like a tactical map, fog rolling off Puget Sound in predictable patterns that won't interfere with my sight lines. Dawn breaks gray and quiet, exactly how surveillance should operate. The familiar taste of black coffee gone cold coats my tongue while morning dampness seeps through my tactical gear.

Silence means safety. Always has.

The target building sits three blocks east, its windows reflecting early morning light like mirror shields. Standard corporate architecture housing non-standard business—the third-floor office where arms dealer Drazen Kostic conducts transactions he believes stay private.

Six hours of observation. The patterns are clear. Security rotates every ninety minutes. Delivery entrance is unmonitored between shifts. Executive garage accessible through maintenance tunnels.

My scope tracks movement through the windows—Kostic's bodyguard checking the perimeter with the lazy confidence of a man who's never been properly hunted, a secretary arriving early with her predictable vanilla latte, the normal rhythms of a criminal enterprise disguised as legitimate business. Everything proceeds according to established patterns until my encrypted phone vibrates against my ribs.

Once. Ghost.

Only Mason uses that protocol.

But first, unfinished business. Yesterday's recon included some practice fun. Clay pigeon on Kostic's roof, precisely 847 meters out. The perfect distance for maintaining skills during mind-numbing surveillance.

Wind speed: minimal.

Temperature: steady.

Humidity: acceptable.

The Barrett .50 caliber settles against my shoulder with familiar weight, cold metal warming under my grip. The scope's reticle finds the small orange target perched on the distant building's edge, a bright spot against the gray Seattle morning.

At this distance, physics matters. Bullet flight time: 1.2 seconds. Not shooting where the target is—calculating where it'll be when death arrives.

Breathe in. Breathe out. Natural respiratory pause. Heartbeat minimal. Smooth trigger squeeze.

The rifle kicks. Thunder rolls across the waterfront. 1.2 seconds later, orange fragments explode against the sky.

Better than shooting people. Less satisfying than eliminating genuine threats. At least clay pigeons don't require paperwork.

Phone still buzzing. Mason hates waiting.

"What?"

"Need you in D.C. Protection detail." Mason's voice carries that particular edge, meaning immediate deployment. "Linguistics professor. Potential Phoenix target."

Phoenix.

The name alone spikes adrenaline. Since Ryan and Celeste's staged deaths three months ago, Phoenix adapted. Evolved. New protocols. Enhanced surveillance. Bodies are stacking up among those investigating its operations.

My jaw clenches hard enough to crack molars. Protecting academics ranks below dental surgery on my preference scale. University types never shut up. Questions. Explanations. Theories. Endless noise compromising operational security.

"When?"

"Yesterday. Her name's Dr. Eliza Wren. Georgetown University. Smart enough to decode something she shouldn't have."

Georgetown. Historic district with narrow streets designed for horses, not tactical vehicles. Medieval building layouts favoring siege defense over modern protection protocols. Tourist crowds providing both cover and complications.

Tactical nightmare.

"Threat?"

"Three researchers working on similar projects. All dead within two weeks. Morrison called from the FBI, and we've confirmed Phoenix activated the Obsidian protocol."

Obsidian. Phoenix's cleanup protocol. Professional teams. Military-grade equipment. Zero witnesses.

If Obsidian targets this professor, she has intelligence Phoenix considers existentially threatening.

"On it."

My equipment disappears into tactical bags with movements honed through six years in Delta Force, four years with Cerberus. Weapons, surveillance gear, communications, and medical supplies. Everything needed for hostile territory deployment. The metallic smell of gun oil mingles with leather and cordite—the scent of my profession.

"Charter will pick you up at the airport. No need to mention speed is of the essence."

And yet, Mason did mention it. Spending words like they're going out of style.

"Copy that."

The drive to Sea-Tac provides time for tactical planning. Time to Reagan National—about five hours. Reagan National to Georgetown—forty minutes with traffic. My old Cerberus safe house in Columbia Heights—twenty minutes from campus, stocked with heavier weapons than TSA allows.

It's a necessary stop, which means my arrival at Georgetown will be after 2300 hours.

Dr. Eliza Wren's file spreads across my tablet. PhD in linguistics from Harvard. Former DoD encryption specialist. Current Georgetown professor specializing in ancient cipher analysis. Published extensively on pattern recognition, historical cryptography, and evolutionary linguistics.

Intelligence suggests she stumbled across Phoenix communications while researching Roman military codes.

Her academic curiosity comes with lethal consequences.

Her photo stops me cold.

Not the expected middle-aged academic with thick glasses and gray hair. Dr. Wren appears early thirties, with shoulder-length auburn hair framing an intelligent face. Green eyes behind stylish frames. High cheekbones. Full lips. The kind of understated beauty that suggests she prioritizes intellectual pursuits over physical appearance.

Gorgeous. Absolutely fucking gorgeous.

The kind of woman who'd make me look twice in a bar, worth crossing a crowded room to buy drinks for. On paper, she's everything I avoid—another academic with soft hands and too many questions. But this photo? Prime fucking material. I can see it perfectly—cornering her in some bar bathroom, lifting her onto the sink, those intellectual eyes going wide when she realizes I'm not asking permission. Hands tangled in that auburn hair, fucking her against cold tile until all those fancy words disappear, until that clever mouth can't form theories or questions, just my name. Maybe not even that. Pure physical connection where her PhD means nothing and she's just soft skin, all need and heat.

No names. No history. No future.

Perfect relationship material if relationships involved nothing beyond fucking and mutual orgasms.

Unfortunately, this assignment requires keeping her alive, not keeping her quiet through more enjoyable methods.

My phone buzzes with updated intelligence from Mason. Phoenix is moving fast on this one. Its Obsidian protocol means complete elimination—no witnesses, no evidence, no survivors. Phoenix will have already identified her contacts, mapped her routines, and isolated her from any support networks. Standard Phoenix tactics since Ryan and Celeste—systematic, thorough, lethal.

A storm system forces our flight path north, adding forty minutes. We finally touch down at Reagan National at 2237 hours.

If she's still alive, it's a miracle.

Rental car paperwork. Agonizing bureaucracy. Insurance options. GPS upgrades. Fuel packages. Each declining second potentially costs her life. Finally mobile at 2308 hours, I navigate D.C.'s familiar streets toward Columbia Heights. The city smells of rain and exhaust, monuments lit against darkness like beacons of democracy Phoenix seeks to undermine.

The safe house remains undisturbed. Electronic locks untriggered. Dust patterns confirm no recent entry. The weapons cache provides essential upgrades—body armor, additional magazines, tactical communications gear, and night vision equipment. The familiar weight of proper armament settles across my frame.

2341 hours when I finally approach Georgetown University.

The medieval architecture appears exactly as remembered—

historic buildings cramped together, insufficient parking, narrow streets designed before automobiles existed. Stone walls still radiating the day's heat into the cool October night. Student laughter carries from nearby bars, the normal sounds of university life proceeding while death hunts one of their professors.

Dr. Wren's office location—Healy Hall, third floor, Linguistics department—glows with light despite the late hour.

Still working.

Still alive.

She remains visible through her office windows, silhouette bent over her desk, completely absorbed in her work. A perfect target for anyone with long-range capabilities. Any operator with basic training would have closed those blinds, varied their routine, and maintained some situational awareness. However, academics tend to think in theoretical terms rather than physical ones.

Movement catches my peripheral vision. Black SUV. Government plates. Three occupants proceeding slowly toward the building. Not university security. Not local law enforcement. Professional operators conducting reconnaissance.

The Phoenix advance team.

Encrypted line to Mason. "Phoenix on site. Three operators. Advance reconnaissance. Target still in her office."

"Copy. Do what you must. Keep her alive."

The SUV completes its circuit—taking note of security cameras, patrol routes, and civilian patterns. Professional assessment before the strike. They'll return with a full tactical team once reconnaissance confirms the target location and optimal approach vectors.

Standard military planning adapted for assassination.

Nine operators for one academic?

No sniper taking position for a clean shot through those wide-open windows? They're moving for breach and clear, not elimination. From 200 meters, I could put a round through her temple before she finished typing her next sentence. Any competent marksman could. Phoenix has competent marksmen.

Which means they need her alive. At least initially.

Information extraction. They want to know what she found, who she told, and where the evidence is stored. Then they'll kill her and make it look accidental. Another professor having a mental breakdown. Suicide by hanging, maybe. Or prescription overdose. Something that fits the narrative of an overworked academic who stumbled onto something that terrified her.

Changes the tactical situation completely. They'll use non-lethal methods—tasers, tranquilizers, physical restraint. Gives me an advantage. They're planning for capture. I'm planning for war.

At 2345 hours, the situation escalates dramatically. The black SUV returns, accompanied by two additional vehicles. Nine operators deploy with the kind of professional equipment that means business. A full Phoenix tactical team assembling for Obsidian protocol implementation. Dr. Eliza Wren has approximately ten minutes to live unless I intervene now.

I run through my equipment one final time: sidearm, tactical knife, communications gear, medical supplies. It's insufficient firepower for a sustained engagement against nine operators, but adequate for an extraction if I prioritize speed over confrontation.

The team establishes its perimeter. Two operators cover the main entrance, while another pair takes care of the service corridors. One maintains overwatch from across the quad. The remaining four prepare for entry, stacking up exactly as trained. It's textbook deployment for eliminating an isolated target who has no idea death is climbing her stairs.

Time to move.

My approach through the campus landscaping provides

concealment until the final fifty meters. The smell of freshly cut grass mingles with the crisp, damp air of autumn leaves on the October night. Phoenix operators cover all ground-level entrances. Vertical infiltration becomes my only option.

Gothic architecture favors climbers—decorative stonework creates natural handholds, window ledges offer footholds, and architectural flourishes provide grip that modern buildings lack. The north face offers a drainage pipe running past a second-floor balcony, continuing to a third-floor window that maintenance, no doubt, never remembers to lock.

My old D.C. knowledge is paying dividends tonight.

The pipe holds my weight easily, decades of paint and rust providing unexpected grip. I climb hand over hand, using window ledges as foot placements. It's twenty feet to the second-floor balcony, another fifteen to the third-floor window.

Child's play compared to Afghan cliff faces.

The window slides open with barely a whisper—predictable negligence from maintenance. Inside, I find a darkened classroom with chairs stacked for cleaning, the smell of chalk dust and old books heavy in the air.

Sound carries strangely in these old buildings. The Phoenix team ascends the main stairwell two floors below, their tactical boots creating distinctive echoes on the stone steps. They're making no attempt at stealth.

Cocky bastards.

The third-floor corridor stretches ahead under harsh fluorescent lights. Dr. Wren's door is closed, but a thin line of light bleeds beneath it. No sounds emerge from within—no typing, no talking, nothing.

Too quiet. Either she left, or she's hiding.

Phoenix reaches the second floor. Their boots echo in the stairwell, getting closer. Ninety seconds until they reach this level.

I test the doorknob. Locked. These old locks are more suggestion than security—a quick manipulation with my knife and the mechanism clicks open.

The office door swings inward silently, revealing the expected chaos—books stacked like defensive fortifications, papers scattered across every surface, three computer monitors still glowing with data streams. The air carries the smell of cold coffee and vanilla perfume. The desk chair sits empty, pushed back from the keyboard.

But she's here. The faint sound of panicked breathing comes from beneath the desk, rapid and shallow.

She's hiding as if ducking under furniture will stop professional killers.

Phoenix footsteps on the stairs. Sixty seconds.

I reach under the desk, my hand finding fabric.

I pull.

She comes out swinging, a wild haymaker catching my jaw with surprising force. Pure panic drives her fists as she fights for her life.

"No no no no—"

My hand covers her mouth, cutting off the stream of negatives. Her eyes go wide behind those glasses, green like sea glass, tears starting to form.

"Cerberus Security." The words are quick, quiet, and whispered directly into her ear. "Morrison sent me."

Recognition flickers through the panic. Not Phoenix. Rescue. Her body stops fighting and goes limp, nearly dropping to the floor.

I catch her, steadying her against my chest. She's soft against the tactical vest, and that vanilla scent is stronger up close. Fuck.

Focus. Mission first.

"Can you run?"

She nods against my hand.

"Stay quiet. Move when I move. Stop when I stop. Understand?"

Another nod. I release her mouth.

"Thank God, I thought—Morrison said someone was coming but—are you really—who are you—"

Hand back over her mouth. "Quiet. Now."

Phoenix is on the third floor. Thirty seconds.

She's already talking. Already asking questions. Already compromising operational security with her inability to shut the fuck up.

This extraction just became my personal nightmare. A chatty academic who can't stop verbalizing every thought while professional killers hunt us through a hostile city.

Fucking perfect.

THREE

Eliza

FIRST CONTACT

A HAND GRABS MY ARM FROM ABOVE—STRONG, CALLOUSED, uncompromising.

I'm yanked out from under my desk with enough force to send me sprawling, my knees hitting the floor hard enough to bruise. Pure panic drives my fist toward whoever's attacking me, and I connect with something solid—a jaw, maybe—before another hand covers my mouth, cutting off my stream of "No no no no—"

"Cerberus Security." The words are quiet, controlled, and whispered directly in my ear. Male voice. Deep. Authoritative. "Morrison sent me."

Morrison. FBI. Help, not harm.

My body goes limp with relief so suddenly I nearly collapse, but strong hands steady me against what feels like a tactical vest. The man holding me smells like gun oil and soap, something woodsy underneath, and he's solid as a wall. Warm. Alive. Here to save me, not kill me.

He releases my mouth, and I finally get a clear look at my rescuer.

Oh. Oh my.

He's tall—easily six-two—with dark hair and the most intense green eyes I've ever seen. Not the kind of green you find in nature, but something deeper, more dangerous. Arctic ice over deep water. The fluorescent lights cast shadows across his face, highlighting cheekbones that could cut glass and a jaw that belongs on ancient statuary.

He stands with perfect stillness, that kind of controlled readiness I've only seen in documentary footage of special forces operators. Every line of his body radiates coiled power—broad shoulders filling out a tactical vest, arms that clearly know their way around a weight room, thighs that—I should not be noticing his thighs right now.

But I am. God help me, I am.

My gaze drops lower before I can stop it, and heat floods my cheeks. The impressive bulge behind his tactical pants has nothing to do with weapons or equipment. Everything about him screams dominant male, from the way he holds himself to the careful control in every movement.

He looks exactly like my fantasies. The gladiator who wouldn't ask permission. The warrior who'd simply take. The kind of man who could make me stop talking with just a look— or better methods.

"Can you run?" His voice cuts through my inappropriate cataloging of his physical attributes.

I nod, not trusting my voice yet.

"Stay quiet. Move when I move. Stop when I stop. Understand?"

Another nod. He releases me fully, and I immediately miss the contact. Which is insane. People are trying to kill me, and I'm having absurdly sexual thoughts about my rescuer.

"Thank God, I thought—Morrison said someone was

coming but—are you really—who are you—are those real guns—"

His hand covers my mouth again. "Quiet. Now."

The footsteps in the hallway are getting closer. Heavy boots. Multiple sets. They're almost at my door.

He pulls me behind him, positioning his body between me and the door. One hand moves to his weapon while the other keeps me pressed against the wall. His body heat radiates through the tactical vest, and despite everything, I notice the solid wall of muscle protecting me.

The doorknob rattles. They're checking if it's locked.

He guides me silently toward the back corner of my office where an old supply closet door connects to the adjacent classroom. I'd forgotten it existed, hidden behind a filing cabinet. How does he know the building layout better than I do?

We slip through just as the main door splinters open. He eases the closet door shut behind us, and we're plunged into musty darkness that smells like old textbooks and dust. Through the thin door, I hear boots storming into my office.

"Empty. Target's not here." A harsh male voice, accent I can't place.

"Check the computers. See what she was working on."

His hand finds mine in the darkness, squeezing once. A signal to move. We creep through the connecting classroom, my heels impossibly loud on the old wooden floor despite my attempts to walk on my toes. Every step sounds like thunder to my ears.

"Where are we going—who were those men—is Morrison okay—why do they want me dead—"

"Quiet," he breathes against my ear, and the warmth of his breath sends an inappropriate shiver down my spine.

We reach the classroom door. He checks the hallway, then pulls me out and to the left, away from my office. His hand on my lower back guides me with gentle pressure—turn here, faster now, stop. It's like a dance where only he knows the steps.

The Gothic architecture of Georgetown, which has always felt like home, now feels like a maze. These stone walls that sheltered my academic pursuits suddenly seem to close in. The narrow hallways that once felt cozy now trap us with limited escape routes.

Behind us, shouting. They've discovered we're not in my office.

Without warning, he yanks the fire alarm on the wall. The piercing shriek makes me jump, instinctively pressing closer to him.

"Chaos," he says simply. "Misdirection."

Of course. The alarm will force any remaining security to investigate, and the men who are after me will have to account for emergency responders. It buys us time and confusion.

He pulls me through a door marked "Authorized Personnel Only." The maintenance corridor beyond is narrow, forcing us closer together. Exposed pipes run along the ceiling, and the air smells of industrial cleaner and dust. The fire alarm is muffled here but still audible, adding urgency to our movement.

"Who are you?" The questions pour out despite his earlier command. "Cerberus Security, like the three-headed dog that guards the underworld? Is that supposed to be reassuring? Because mythologically speaking, Cerberus isn't exactly friendly. He prevents the dead from leaving, which technically makes him more of a prison guard than a protector, and—"

He stops so abruptly that I collide with his back. Solid. Warm. Immovable.

He turns in the narrow space, and suddenly we're face-to-face, inches apart. Those green eyes bore into mine with an intensity that steals my breath. This close, I can see flecks of gold in the green, the faint shadow of stubble along his jaw, the way his mouth—

"Dr. Wren." His voice is low, controlled, but holds an edge. "Nine professional killers from an organization called Phoenix are hunting you through this building. They want to extract information about what you decoded, then kill you and make it look like suicide. We need to move fast and silent. So for the love of God, shut up."

The words are harsh, but something in his expression isn't. I see respect there, mixed with frustration and something else—awareness. The same awareness that's making my skin tingle everywhere he's almost touching me.

I open my mouth to respond—probably to explain that verbal processing is actually a recognized cognitive strategy and that suppressing it could impair my ability to think clearly—

His finger presses against my lips. Warm. Calloused. Gentle despite everything.

"Please," he says, and something about that single word, the way his voice drops when he says it, makes me nod.

For the first time in my adult life, I actually want to be quiet. Not because I have nothing to say—my mind is racing with a thousand questions and observations—but because this man, this dangerous stranger who smells like violence and safety combined, told me to.

That realization terrifies me more than the killers hunting us through Georgetown's Gothic halls. I've never obeyed anyone's commands, never wanted to surrender control, but something about his absolute authority makes me want to comply.

He removes his finger from my lips slowly, his eyes tracking the movement. The air between us crackles with tension that has nothing to do with Phoenix and everything to do with the way we're looking at each other.

Then distant shouting breaks the spell. Phoenix is systematically searching the building despite the fire alarm chaos.

"Move."

His command shocks me, and I instantly obey.

He leads me deeper into the maintenance corridors, through a confusing series of turns that have me completely lost. The passages seem to run between the building's walls, probably original to the construction. The air gets colder, damper, and I realize we're heading down.

"The basement?" I whisper, proud of myself for managing just two words.

He nods, approval flickering in his eyes. Maybe I can learn to be quiet after all.

We descend narrow metal stairs that creak under our weight. The basement is a maze of mechanical rooms, storage areas, and the building's heating system. Massive boilers hum and clank, creating enough noise to mask our movement.

He leads me to what looks like a maintenance closet but opens to reveal another passage—this one leading to the utility tunnels that run beneath campus. The entrance is hidden behind a false panel that he seems to know exactly how to open.

"How do you know about—"

His look silences me more effectively than his hand ever could. Right. Quiet.

The tunnel is concrete, cylindrical, maybe six feet in diameter. Pipes and cables run along the curved walls. It smells of earth and dampness and age. He guides me inside, his hand on my elbow steady and sure.

We move about thirty feet in, far enough that the entrance is barely visible in the darkness behind us. There's a metal grate here, part of the tunnel's original construction, designed to section off maintenance areas. He pulls it across behind us with a metallic scrape that echoes in the confined space. He produces a length of wire from one of his vest pockets and secures it in place.

To a casual search, we're behind a locked maintenance barrier. To a thorough search—well, hopefully Phoenix won't be that thorough. Not down here in the dark.

"We wait here," he says, voice barely audible.

"How long?" I manage just two words again. Look at me, learning.

"Dawn."

That's it. One word. But I understand. Phoenix will search all night, but daylight brings witnesses—students, faculty, campus security. They'll have to pull back or risk exposure. In darkness, we're hunted. In daylight, we might have a chance.

I slide down the curved wall to sit on the cold concrete. He remains standing, alert, weapon ready. Protecting me even though he doesn't know me, even though I can't stop talking, even though I'm probably the worst person to protect in the history of protection details.

"Why?" I ask, then bite my lip. One word. That's progress.

He looks down at me, and something in his expression softens fractionally. "It's what I do."

Four words. More than I expected.

I pull my knees to my chest, wrapping my arms around them. The motion makes me smaller, and I see his jaw tighten. He shrugs out of his jacket—not the tactical vest, but a black jacket over it—and drapes it around my shoulders without a word.

It smells like him. Gun oil and soap and danger.

It smells like safety.

For now, in this tunnel beneath Georgetown, with killers hunting above and dawn hours away, I'm safe. Because this man won't let anything happen to me.

I just have to learn to stop talking long enough to stay alive.

The hardest challenge of my life, and it has nothing to do with the PhD I earned or the code I cracked.

It has everything to do with trusting this silent warrior who makes me want to be quiet just to hear him breathe.

FOUR

Cooper

UNDERGROUND

THE TUNNEL'S CONCRETE CURVES FORCE US INTO UNNATURAL positions. Can't stand. Can't stretch out. Just exist in this six-foot diameter pipe while Phoenix hunts above.

She shifts against the wall, trying to find comfort that doesn't exist. The movement pulls her sweater tight across her chest, and I force my eyes away. Focus on the mission. Not on how her jeans hug curves that belong in fantasies, not protection details.

The emergency lighting from the basement barely reaches us here, casting everything in shadow. Just enough light to see her face, the stubborn set of her jaw, the way auburn hair falls around her shoulders. The dim glow catches highlights in those waves, making me want to wrap the strands around my fist.

Fuck. Even in a utility tunnel, she's gorgeous.

The confined space means her scent fills every breath—vanilla from whatever she uses in her hair, something clean and feminine underneath. Close enough that when she shifts position, her knee brushes mine. Close enough to see the green of her eyes behind those stylish glasses when she looks at me.

Bad idea. Very bad fucking idea.

"So we just sit here?" Her voice echoes slightly in the tunnel. "For six hours? In this freezing pipe?"

"Yes."

"That's your whole plan? Hide and wait?"

"Alive is better than dead."

She pulls her knees up, wrapping her arms around them. The position makes her look smaller, but also does interesting things to her already impressive cleavage. Voluptuous. That's the word. Full breasts that would overflow my hands, hips made for gripping.

Professional distance. Right.

"I need answers," she says, because of course she does. "What exactly is Phoenix? Is this connected to what happened to Sarah, David, and Lisa?"

The questions pour out rapid-fire. Typical academic—needs to understand, analyze, categorize every piece of information. Can't just sit quietly and wait for extraction.

"Phoenix is a military AI targeting system. Supposedly shut down. Actually privatized. Now it kills anyone it considers a threat."

"What counts as a threat?" She pauses, eyes closing briefly, then corrects herself. "Who does it count as a threat?"

Smart woman. Even terrified, she's thinking.

"Anyone investigating it."

"Privatized by whom?"

"Unknown."

"Unknown? That's not an answer."

"It's the only answer."

Her frustration radiates across the small space between us. She shifts again, and her shoulder bumps mine. Warm. Soft. Dangerous.

"I'm not some helpless victim you need to manage," she says, fire flashing in those green eyes. "I'm a former DoD encryption specialist with top secret clearance. I can handle the truth."

The DoD background explains the sharp questions. The rapid threat assessment. Also explains why Phoenix wants her dead—she has the skills to decode their communications.

"The truth is, we don't know who controls Phoenix. Could be defense contractors. Shadow government. Private military. The system covers its tracks."

"But you're investigating it."

"No. I'm protecting someone Phoenix wants dead. Big difference."

"What do you mean by big difference?"

"My job is keeping you alive. You stay alive by doing what I say when I say it. And keeping your mouth shut when I tell you to."

Her jaw clenches. "Are you always this bossy?"

"Yes."

"You're an ass."

"You're alive."

She huffs out a breath that might be frustration or amusement. Hard to tell in the dark. "We're not here to be friends, I get it. But we're stuck in this pipe for the foreseeable future. We might as well talk."

"Talking makes noise. Noise attracts attention."

"From who? We're in a sealed tunnel behind a locked grate thirty feet from the entrance. You said they won't search down here."

Valid point. Annoying, but valid.

"What do you want to know?"

"Everything. Start with who you really are. I don't even know your name. Are you military? Ex-military? Private contractor? How long have you been doing this? Why this job? Why protection work?"

Jesus Christ. The woman can't stop asking questions even when her life depends on silence.

"Cooper McKenzie." The name feels formal in the confined space. "Former Delta Force. Six years. Cerberus Security. Four years. Protection because it pays. This job because Mason assigned it."

"That's your autobiography? Twenty one words?"

"Covers the basics."

"It covers nothing! What's your specialty? Weapons? Demolitions? Communications? Where have you operated? What made you leave Delta? Who's Mason? What kind of—"

"Stop."

She blinks at the command. "Stop, what?"

"Talking."

"But—"

"Phoenix teams are still in the building. Sound carries through pipes. You want to broadcast our position?"

Not entirely true. The mechanical systems create enough white noise to mask normal conversation. But if she keeps talking, I might do something stupid. Like notice how her lips move when she forms words. Or how she gestures with her hands even in the confined space. Or how her breath catches when she gets excited about a topic.

All dangerous observations.

She falls silent, but I can practically hear her brain working. Cataloging information. Forming new questions. Planning her next verbal assault.

She makes a small sound that might be indignation or amusement. But she stops talking. For about thirty seconds.

"How long have we been down here?"

I check my watch. "Forty-three minutes."

"So five hours and seventeen minutes to go."

"If you're going to count down every minute—"

"I'm not. I'm just—processing. This is how I handle stress. I talk. I analyze. I question. It's who I am."

"It's going to get you killed."

She pulls back slightly to look at me. In the dim light, her eyes are more gray than green. "You really think they'll find us down here?"

"If you keep talking? Yes."

"You're just saying that to shut me up."

"Is it working?"

"No."

Despite everything, my mouth twitches. Almost a smile. She's terrified, hunted, trapped in a tunnel with a stranger, and still she pushes back. Still she questions. Still she refuses to be silenced.

Stubborn woman.

"Tell me about the code," I say, partly for intelligence and partly to give her something to focus on besides fear.

Her entire demeanor changes. She straightens, eyes lighting up behind those glasses. "It's fascinating, actually. I was analyzing frequency patterns in Roman military dispatches when I noticed anomalies. The mathematical distribution was all wrong for ancient encryption. Too sophisticated. Too—modern."

She launches into an explanation involving algorithms, frequency analysis, and pattern recognition. Most of it goes over my head, but her passion is clear. This is her element—solving puzzles, finding patterns, understanding the incomprehensible.

"So you cracked Phoenix's communication system by accident?"

"Not cracked. Not entirely. I found fragments. Enough to know someone was using our historical research as camouflage for modern encryption. But the full code ..." She shakes her head. "I'd need more time. More data."

"Time you don't have."

"Because Phoenix wants me dead." The fear creeps back into

her voice. "An AI decided I'm a threat and sent killers after me. How is that even legal?"

"It's not."

"Then why doesn't someone stop it?"

"We're trying."

"We?"

"Cerberus. Others. People who know what Phoenix really is."

She's quiet for a moment, processing. Then, "Have you faced Phoenix before?"

The question hits unexpectedly. Memories of Ryan and Celeste, of operations gone wrong, of an AI that adapts and learns and never stops hunting.

"Yes."

"Did everyone survive?"

"No."

She tenses against me. "Oh."

Silence stretches between us. Real silence this time, heavy with implication. Above us, through layers of concrete and steel, Phoenix teams continue their hunt. But down here, in our cold bubble of temporary safety, there's just us.

"I'm scared," she admits quietly.

"Good."

"Good?"

"Fear keeps you alive. Makes you careful. Makes you listen when I tell you to move."

"Is that why you're so …" She waves a hand vaguely. "Intense?"

Perceptive. Too perceptive.

"What are you afraid of?"

Failing. Losing another client. Watching someone die because I wasn't fast enough, smart enough, careful enough. But those aren't things you say out loud.

"Phoenix."

"Liar."

The word hangs between us. She's right, of course. Phoenix is just a system. The fear runs deeper—fear of failure, of loss, of not being enough when it counts.

"Everyone's afraid of something," she continues. "I'm afraid of dying before I finish my research. Of never understanding the full pattern. Of being silenced before I can share what I've learned."

"You're afraid of being quiet."

She laughs—soft, surprised. "Yes. I suppose I am. Silence feels like surrender."

"Sometimes silence is survival."

"Is that what you tell yourself? When you don't talk about whatever haunts you?"

Too fucking perceptive.

"We're not talking about me."

"Why not? We have five hours to kill."

"Because my history won't keep you alive."

"But it might help me understand you. And since my life is literally in your hands, I'd like to know more than your name and former employer."

She has a point. But talking about Syria, about failures and ghosts and the weight of command decisions—that's not happening. Not with her. Not with anyone.

"Ask something else."

She considers, still pressed against my side for warmth. "Why protection work? You could do anything with your skill set. Private military, corporate security, consulting. Why choose to protect people?"

The honest answer is complicated. Protection is penance. Keeping others alive because I couldn't keep my team alive. But that's too much truth for a tunnel conversation with a stranger.

"It's straightforward. Clear objectives. Keep the client alive."

"That's it? No deeper meaning?"

"Sometimes a job is just a job."

"I don't believe you."

"Doesn't matter what you believe."

She makes that sound again—frustration mixed with something else. "You're impossible."

"You're exhausting."

"Match made in heaven then."

The words hang in the air, and she immediately tenses. "I didn't mean—that came out wrong—I just meant we're obviously incompatible, not that we're matched, and definitely not—"

"Dr. Wren."

"Yes?"

"Stop talking."

"Right. Okay. Stopping now."

She lasts maybe ninety seconds.

"But seriously, how are we getting out of here when dawn comes?"

FIVE

Cooper

BODY HEAT

She absorbs my limited information with the same intensity she probably applies to ancient language patterns. She scans my face, cataloging details, searching for additional data.

"My colleagues who were killed—Sarah Williams, David Kim, Lisa Parker—did Phoenix murder them?"

"Yes."

"Can you answer anything with more than one word?"

"Obsidian protocol."

She shakes her head and rolls her eyes, puffing out a breath that moves the hair falling across her forehead.

"Great. Two words. One more than one."

Despite the circumstances, watching her get riled up is entertaining as hell. The way her cheeks flush with frustration, the spark in those green eyes—I'm getting a kick out of pushing her buttons.

"I know that word. Obsidian. It appeared in several of the coded files I found. I thought it was a codename, but it's not. What is it?"

"It is a codename."

"For what?" As her exasperation grows, my interest increases. There's something sexy about her the more frustrated she gets. She's smart. Too fucking smart for her own good.

"Phoenix kill protocol."

"How many people has Obsidian killed?"

"Nobody knows."

She's quiet for several minutes, processing this information. The basement's mechanical systems hum around us—heating pipes clicking, ventilation fans cycling, electrical systems humming their constant background noise.

Above us, the fire alarm finally stops. Emergency vehicles arrive on campus, sirens wailing. Phoenix teams will blend into the chaos, pose as concerned security personnel responding to the threat.

Professional. Disciplined. Patient.

"Cooper?"

"Yeah."

"Are we going to die down here?"

The question comes out small and vulnerable. She's finally hit the wall—the moment when the reality of her situation penetrates her academic curiosity and hits pure survival instinct.

"No."

"How can you be so certain?"

"Because I'm very good at keeping people alive."

She shifts against the tunnel wall, trying to find a comfortable position that doesn't exist.

"Can you tell me about Cerberus? How did you know how to find me? Why are you helping people fight Phoenix?"

"We're a private military contractor specializing in protection services. Got the call yesterday."

"From whom?"

"Ghost."

"Ghost?"

"My boss."

"His real name is Ghost?"

"Mason Blackwood. We call him Ghost."

"Military nicknames?"

"Yes."

"What's your nickname?"

The question catches me off guard. Most clients don't care about team dynamics or operational details. They want protection, extraction, and survival. Dr. Eliza Wren wants to understand everything.

"Whisper."

"Whisper?" Her eyebrows shoot up. "You? Mr. Monosyllabic Grunts and Single-Word Answers? I'd think they'd call you Caveman."

Despite the circumstances, her reaction almost makes me smile. Almost.

"Sniper. Move quietly. Strike silently."

"Ah." She nods as if this explains everything. "So you're the team's long-range specialist."

"Among other things."

"What other things?"

"Surveillance. Reconnaissance. Target elimination."

"Target elimination." She repeats the words carefully. "You mean assassination."

"When necessary."

Most people flinch when they learn what I do for a living. Dr. Eliza Wren just nods and moves on to the next question.

"How many people are on your team?"

"Five active. Two inactive."

"What happened to the inactive members?"

Ryan and Celeste's situation is classified, but explaining it requires more words than I prefer using. "Phoenix. Had to disappear."

"They're alive?"

"Yes."

"But they can't come back?"

"Not while Phoenix exists."

Understanding flashes across her features. "So this is personal for your team."

"Everything's personal when Phoenix is involved."

She shifts again, pulling her knees closer to her chest. Her lips show the first hint of blue, and her hands shake slightly as she rubs her arms.

Time for a tactical adjustment.

The temperature down here hovers around fifty degrees. Concrete leaches heat from anything it touches. She's already shivering slightly, arms wrapped around herself. The jacket I gave her helps, but not enough.

"You're cold," I observe.

"I'm fine."

"You're shivering."

"It's fifty degrees in a concrete pipe. Of course I'm shivering. Basic thermodynamics. The human body maintains a core temperature of 98.6 degrees Fahrenheit. In an environment this cold, without proper insulation, heat loss occurs through conduction to the concrete, convection in the air, and radiation—"

"Come here."

She stops mid-lecture. "What?"

"Body heat. Basic survival."

"You want me to—cuddle with you? For warmth?"

"Unless you prefer hypothermia."

She stares at me in the dim light, probably weighing her options. Freeze slowly over six hours or share body heat with a virtual stranger who makes her nervous.

Survival wins.

She scoots closer, tentatively at first. The tunnel's curve forces her to lean against my side. I shift to accommodate her, creating a pocket of warmth between my body and the wall.

"This is purely for survival," she says.

"Obviously."

"I don't want you getting any ideas."

"Wouldn't dream of it."

But when she settles against me, her head fitting perfectly against my shoulder, her warmth seeping through my tactical vest, ideas are exactly what I'm getting. Bad ones. Unprofessional ones. The kind that involve finding out what sounds she makes when she's not talking. What it would take to make her speechless.

Her hair tickles my jaw. That vanilla scent is stronger now, mixed with adrenaline and fear and something uniquely her. Despite everything—the danger, the cold, the concrete—she feels right pressed against me.

Which is fucked up on multiple levels.

"Better?" I ask.

"Warmer," she admits. Then, because she can't help herself: "Did you know the phrase 'body heat' is actually redundant? All heat is technically body heat in the sense that it's energy produced by matter, and in thermodynamics—"

"Dr. Wren."

"Yes?"

"Shut up." Those green eyes flash with irritation.

"Don't order me around."

Stubborn woman. "It's not an order. It's a tactical necessity."

"Everything's tactical with you, isn't it?"

"When it comes to keeping you alive, everything I tell you to do, you consider it an order and obey instantly. Don't ask questions. Do what I say when I say it."

Her breath catches slightly, and something shifts in her expression. Despite her verbal protests, her body language tells a different story—the way her lips part, the slight dilation of her pupils, the unconscious lean forward.

She responds to authority.

To dominance.

Shit.

Interesting as hell, considering I prefer women who submit in bed. The thought of having her underneath me, responding to commands with breathless obedience instead of endless questions, sends heat straight to my groin.

Wouldn't that be fun?

Fuck. Lock it down.

The metal surface provides marginally more warmth than concrete, but not enough to matter.

"There. Happy now?"

Her shoulder brushes mine as she settles into position, and the contact sends electricity straight through my system. She smells even better up close—vanilla and something distinctly feminine that makes me want to bury my face in her hair.

Professional distance. Maintain professional fucking distance.

But sitting beside me isn't how you conserve body heat effectively. The concrete floor will continue leaching warmth from her body through her jeans.

"Better." I lean forward and wrap my arm around her shoulders, pulling her basically into my lap. "Get your ass off the concrete."

She squirms and tries to push away. "What are you doing?"

"Body heat conservation. Stop fighting me."

She continues to struggle against my grip, and my jaw clenches with frustration.

"That's an order."

Immediately, she goes still. Her body relaxes against mine, that unconscious response to authority surfacing again. Another tell. Another piece of evidence that Dr. Eliza Wren responds to dominance whether she admits it or not.

Which is going to be a really big fucking problem, because now she's sitting directly on my lap, her ass pressed against my cock, which is starting to respond to having a beautiful woman positioned exactly where I want her.

"How is this going to help you conserve body heat?"

"Don't worry about me. I can handle it."

She settles against me, and some of the tension leaves her shoulders as warmth starts transferring between us. Her brain's working again, processing the situation.

"Phoenix is a robot that kills people."

"AI. Not a robot."

"Thank you for that crucial distinction." Sarcasm drips from every word. "I feel much better knowing it's artificial intelligence trying to kill me instead of mechanical assassins."

Despite everything, the corner of my mouth twitches. She's got a sharp tongue when she's irritated.

"Cooper?"

"Yeah."

"Are you married?"

The question comes out of nowhere, catching me completely off guard. "What?"

"Married. Girlfriend. Significant other. Someone who worries when you disappear on protection details."

"No."

"Ever been married?"

"No."

"Long-term relationships?"

"No."

"Why not?"

Because I prefer quick hookups in bars where no names are exchanged. No questions about seeing each other again. Just fuck someone, scratch the itch, and walk away clean. Explaining my lifestyle to civilians never works. Most women can't handle what I do for a living. Relationships require emotional availability that my job doesn't allow.

"Job makes it difficult."

"Difficult how?"

"Travel. Danger. Classified work."

"Lots of military personnel maintain relationships."

"Not like this."

She's quiet for several minutes, processing this information with the same thoroughness she applies to ancient ciphers. When she speaks again, her voice is softer.

"It must be lonely."

The observation hits closer to home than expected. Loneliness isn't something I allow myself to think about—it serves no tactical purpose and compromises operational focus.

But sitting in this cold basement with a brilliant, beautiful woman who asks too many questions and smells like vanilla, the word carries more weight than it should.

"Sometimes."

"What about when this is over? When Phoenix is defeated?"

"If Phoenix is defeated."

"When," she corrects firmly. "You said Cerberus fights Phoenix and sometimes wins. That implies you believe victory is possible."

"Victory is possible. Survival isn't guaranteed."

"For me or for you?"

Both. But admitting that reveals more vulnerability than tactical situations allow.

"Focus on getting through tonight."

She's shivering harder now despite our shared body heat.

"I can't stop thinking about Sarah, David, and Lisa. They

were good people. Brilliant researchers. They didn't deserve to die because they were curious about historical patterns."

"No one deserves to die because an AI decides it."

"But especially not academics who stumbled across something accidentally." She leans slightly closer, seeking additional warmth. "How do you do it? How do you live knowing that system is out there killing innocent people?"

"By fighting it."

"Doesn't the futility ever get to you? You said sometimes Phoenix wins. How many people has it killed while you've been fighting it?"

Too many. Far too fucking many.

"Can't save everyone."

"But you try."

"Yes."

"Why?"

Because someone has to. Because letting Phoenix operate without opposition means accepting that artificial intelligence can decide who lives and dies based on algorithmic threat assessment.

Because Dr. Eliza Wren deserves to live long enough to decode whatever ancient mysteries fascinate her brilliant mind.

"Someone has to."

She shifts again, and her ass grinds against my groin. The contact sends heat racing through my system that has nothing to do with shared warmth and everything to do with the way her body moves against mine. My cock hardens immediately, and there's no way she can't feel it pressing against her.

Dangerous territory.

"Cooper?"

"Yeah."

"When you said Phoenix was privatized—that means someone is profiting from these murders, right? Someone is making money by selling assassination services disguised as autonomous AI operations."

Smart. Too fucking smart.

"Probably."

"Who would pay for that kind of service?"

"Anyone with enough money and something to hide."

"Corporations? Governments? Criminal organizations?"

"All of the above."

Her breathing evens out slightly as shared body heat starts making a difference. But she's still shivering, still losing core temperature faster than we can replace it.

Time for another tactical adjustment.

"Closer."

"What?"

"You're still losing heat. Move closer."

"I don't think—"

"Dr. Wren." Her name comes out rough with frustration. "This is about survival, not seduction. Move closer or develop hypothermia. Your choice."

Color floods her cheeks again, but this time she doesn't argue. Her head comes to rest against my shoulder, auburn hair tickling my neck.

The vanilla scent intensifies, mixing with her natural feminine smell in ways that make concentration nearly impossible. Every breath fills my lungs with her; every small movement sends awareness racing through my system.

Fuck. This woman is going to be the death of me.

"Better?"

"Yes." The word comes out muffled against my shoulder. "Thank you."

Professional distance. Maintain professional fucking distance.

But when she relaxes against me, trusting me to keep her warm and safe in this freezing basement while killers hunt us above, something in my chest tightens in ways that have nothing to do with tactics and everything to do with the way she feels in my arms.

"Cooper?"

"Yeah."

"Are we really going to be okay?"

The question comes out small, vulnerable. Fear finally breaking through academic curiosity and stubborn independence. She's scared—terrified—and trying to be brave about it.

My arm comes around her shoulders automatically, pulling her closer against me. The movement positions her more securely against me, sharing more body heat while keeping her within immediate protective reach.

"We're going to be fine."

"Promise?"

Promises in tactical situations are worthless. Too many variables, too many ways for plans to go wrong. But the way she asks —like she needs something to hold onto in the darkness—makes the word come out anyway.

"Promise."

I tighten my arms around her, pulling her close against my chest, tucking her in like she's something precious that needs protecting. She's quiet after that, breathing evening out as exhaustion and the natural crash of adrenaline compete for dominance.

My hand moves to her hair, fingers threading through the auburn strands. I work out the tangles from our crawl through the tunnel, smoothing the silky waves. The motion is soothing, automatic—something I'd do for a lover after sex—if I ever kept one. I've definitely never done this for a client during a protection detail.

Her breathing slows gradually, and only when she starts to doze against my shoulder do I realize what the hell I'm doing.

Shit.

The basement's mechanical systems continue their steady rhythm around us, providing white noise that masks our conversation from any surveillance equipment Phoenix might deploy.

Above us, campus settles into late-night quiet. Emergency responders complete their building sweep, finding no sign of fire or structural damage. Phoenix teams maintain their perimeter surveillance, patient and professional.

Waiting.

Dr. Eliza Wren fits against me like she belongs, warm and soft and trusting. Her breathing slows gradually, fear giving way to exhaustion as her body finally accepts that immediate death isn't imminent.

Four hours until dawn. Four hours of keeping her warm, safe, and alive.

Four hours of fighting the growing certainty that this assignment just became infinitely more complicated than a simple protection detail.

Because somewhere between her stubborn questions and sharp intelligence, between her courage in the face of mortal terror, and the way she smells like vanilla and possibility, Dr. Eliza Wren stopped being just another client.

And that's the most dangerous development of all.

SIX

Eliza

EXPOSED

I wake up pressed against the warmest, most solid surface I've ever encountered, and for a blissful moment, I forget where I am. Cooper's chest rises and falls beneath my cheek in a steady rhythm that's oddly soothing. His arm remains wrapped around me, holding me securely against him even in sleep. The scent of his skin—something woodsy and masculine—fills my senses.

Reality crashes back as the pipes around us clank and hiss. We're still in the utility tunnel beneath Georgetown, hiding from people who want to kill me. But somehow, wrapped in Cooper's arms, the terror of last night feels manageable.

Distant.

His breathing changes, and I realize he's awake. Probably has been for a while, maintaining that protective hold even as consciousness returned.

"Morning," he says quietly, his voice rough.

"Is it morning? I can't tell down here." I don't move away from him immediately. The warmth is too good, and the security of his embrace too comforting to abandon just yet.

"0630. Time to move."

Of course he knows the exact time without checking a watch. The man probably has an internal chronometer.

I reluctantly pull back, immediately missing his warmth as the tunnel's cold air hits my skin. My neck aches from sleeping in an awkward position, and my legs feel stiff from hours on the concrete floor.

"Where exactly are we moving to?"

"Out of here. Then transport." He's already shifting into operational mode, scanning our surroundings with renewed focus. "Phoenix teams rotate shifts at dawn. Window of opportunity."

"What kind of window?"

"The kind that keeps you breathing."

Always so reassuring. I stretch as much as the confined space allows, working out the kinks in my spine. "Do I look as terrible as I feel?"

His steady gaze moves across my face, lingering on my hair, which probably resembles a bird's nest after sleeping in a tunnel. "You look alive. That's what matters."

"Such a charmer." But something in his gaze makes heat flutter in my stomach. Even disheveled and dirty, he's looking at me like I'm something worth protecting. Worth keeping safe.

"Stay here while I check the route." He moves toward the tunnel entrance with that predatory grace that grabs my attention.

"How long?"

"Ten minutes. Maybe fifteen."

The thought of being alone in this cramped space, even briefly, makes my chest tighten. "What if something happens to you?"

He pauses, looking back at me. "Then you wait. The FBI will find you eventually."

"That's your backup plan? Hope the FBI finds me?"

"You have a better idea?"

I don't, which is frustrating. My entire career revolves around solving puzzles. Linguistics and ancient languages are fascinating puzzles, but this situation requires skills I've never developed. Physical survival, tactical thinking, trusting someone else to keep me safe—none of these appear in academic training programs.

"Just—be careful."

Something flickers across his features—surprise, maybe, at my concern for his safety. "Always am."

Then he's gone, disappearing down the tunnel with barely a sound. The silence he leaves behind feels oppressive, thick with all the dangers waiting outside our temporary sanctuary.

I spend the time trying to make myself presentable, finger-combing my hair and brushing dust off my sweater. It's futile. I look like someone who spent the night hiding in a basement tunnel, because that's exactly what I am.

When Cooper returns, he moves with the satisfied confidence of someone whose reconnaissance confirmed his expectations.

"We're clear. No sign of Phoenix personnel. Building's empty except for weekend maintenance."

"So we can just—walk out?"

"With modifications."

Of course. Nothing about this situation could be simple.

He leads me back through the tunnel, and I try not to think about how much easier the crawling is now that I know where we're going. In the basement mechanical room, the fluorescent lights seem blindingly bright after hours in the dim tunnel.

"Bathroom first," he says, nodding toward a door marked Facilities. "Freshen up. Look like a normal person instead of someone who spent the night hiding from killers."

The bathroom is basic—utilitarian fixtures and harsh lighting that reveals exactly how terrible I look. My hair is a disaster, my makeup long gone, and my clothes are wrinkled and dusty. But warm water feels like luxury after the cold tunnel, and I manage to restore some semblance of normalcy to my appearance.

When I emerge, Cooper hands me a Georgetown University sweatshirt, a baseball cap, and sunglasses.

"Where did you get these?"

"Student walking across campus. Offered her two hundred cash for her Georgetown gear."

"You robbed a college student?"

"I bought merchandise from a willing seller. She seemed thrilled with the transaction."

The sweatshirt is oversized and comfortable, the cap fits well enough, and the sunglasses hide most of my face. I catch my reflection in the bathroom mirror—I look like any other Georgetown student heading to weekend class.

"Better?"

"You'll blend in. Ready?"

No. I'm not ready for any of this. But Cooper's calm competence is reassuring, and staying in the basement isn't an option.

"Lead the way."

The route out of Healy Hall takes us through corridors I rarely use, past classrooms and offices I've never visited. Cooper moves with absolute certainty, checking corners and listening at doorways before proceeding. His hand rests casually on his weapon, hidden beneath his jacket but instantly accessible.

Morning sunlight streaming through tall windows feels surreal after our underground night. Campus looks normal—Saturday morning quiet without the usual 6 or 7 a.m. flurry of students rushing to class or grabbing coffee. A few early risers head toward the library or science buildings, probably graduate students with lab work or researchers like me who prefer weekend solitude for deep thinking. If I didn't know better, I'd think yesterday's terror was just a nightmare.

"Rental car's three blocks east," Cooper says as we exit the building."

I fall into step with him. He moves through campus like he belongs here—just another visitor or contractor with business at the university. His awareness never flags, though. Those green eyes of his constantly scan his surroundings, cataloging threats and escape routes.

I try to match his casual alertness, but my academic brain keeps wandering to analysis instead of survival. The linguistic patterns in overheard conversations, the architectural details of buildings we pass, the social dynamics of student groups—everything captures my attention.

Focus, Eliza. People want to kill you. Pay attention to staying alive instead of studying social interactions.

The rental car sits exactly where Cooper said it would, a nondescript sedan with a parking ticket tucked under the windshield wiper. Of course they got a ticket. Even hiding from assassins, bureaucracy finds a way to intrude.

Cooper reaches the car first and performs what I assume is a security check—looking underneath, examining the doors and windows, probably searching for explosives or tracking devices. The routine is both reassuring and terrifying.

I'm standing a few feet away when Cooper suddenly turns and scans the area behind me. His entire demeanor changes, relaxed awareness shifting into lethal focus.

Then his hand shoots out and grabs mine.

"What—"

"Play along if you want to live."

Before I can process his words, he's pulling me against his side, his arm wrapping around my waist with possessive authority. The contact sends electricity through my system, but there's no time to analyze the sensation because he's spinning me to face him, his other hand sliding up to cup the back of my head.

And then he's kissing me.

Not the tentative, hesitant kisses I've experienced with academic colleagues. This is something else entirely—claiming, demanding, completely overwhelming. His mouth moves against mine with the same confidence he applies to everything else, and my brain simply—stops functioning.

His hand at the back of my head controls the angle and depth of the kiss, while his arm around my waist presses me against his body until there's no space between us. I feel every hard plane of his chest, the heat radiating through his clothes, the way his heart pounds against mine. And lower, pressed against my stomach, the unmistakable evidence of his arousal growing harder with each second our bodies remain locked together.

When his tongue sweeps across my bottom lip, seeking entrance, I open for him. The taste of him—something dark, something dangerous—fills my senses. I grip his jacket, partly to steady myself and partly because I never want this to end.

The kiss goes on forever and ends too soon. When he finally pulls back, I'm breathless and dizzy, staring up into those intense green eyes that are watching me with something that looks like satisfaction.

"Phoenix team. Twelve o'clock," he murmurs against my ear, his voice rough. "Two operatives walking past. Keep your head down."

Phoenix. Right. People trying to kill me. The kiss was camouflage, not passion. A necessity to hide me from surveillance.

Except the way his thumb strokes across my cheek suggests it was more than tactics.

"Are they gone?" I whisper.

"Almost." His arm remains around my waist, keeping me pressed against him. "A few more seconds. Grope me this time."

Grope him?

He leans down and kisses me again, slower this time, more deliberate. Where the first kiss was claiming and urgent, this one is explorative—his mouth moving against mine with the patience of a man who's decided to take his time. The intensity hasn't diminished, but there's something deeper here, something that makes my knees go weak.

His lips leave my mouth, travel to my ear. "Either grope me now, or I'm copping a feel of your breasts."

Holy … What the fuck?

When his hand slides up from my waist, I immediately loop my arms around his neck, fingers threading into his dark hair. I lift up on tiptoe, lean into his kiss, meet his passion with my own, and lose myself in the heat building between us. This is what I've fantasized about—being claimed by a warrior, dominated by a man strong enough to simply take what he wants.

And he wants me to grope him.

Sure. I can do that.

I shift my hands down, over his shoulders, around his waist, lower still. Hands splayed against his ass, I yank him against me. At least that was my plan. He's immovable, which means I fall into him and press right against the hard, rigid length of his arousal.

A soft moan escapes my throat, and the sound snaps me back to reality like a bucket of cold water.

Oh God. What am I doing?

I've just thrown myself into kissing a man I barely know, in broad daylight, on a public street, while people are trying to kill me. The realization hits me like a physical blow, and I try to pull back, but his hand at the back of my head keeps me exactly where he wants me.

"Don't pull away. That's an order." His rough command sends liquid heat straight through my core, making my knees go weak and my heart flutter against my ribs. "I'm going to touch your breasts. I have to sell this." The authoritative tone liquefies me from the inside out, and I find myself melting against him instead of resisting.

He spins me slightly until my back hits the car, then leans over me, his body pressing flush against mine. There's no mistaking his arousal now—the hard length of him pressed against my stomach—but he doesn't seem to care about discretion. He just keeps kissing me, pulling me closer, as if this is about much more than keeping me alive. Then his hand cups my breast.

Those seconds stretch into an eternity of being held against Cooper's chest, feeling his strength and warmth, breathing in his scent. When he finally releases me, I feel cold and strangely bereft.

"Clear." He steps back, professional distance returning like a wall between us. "Car. Now."

He opens the door for me. The gesture is so perfectly gentlemanly that it creates a jarring contrast with the warrior who just claimed my mouth like he owned it. He waits while I settle into the seat, then closes the door quietly, as if he hadn't just kissed me senseless against the side of the vehicle.

As he walks around to the driver's side, I catch him glancing at my lips through the windshield. That kiss affected him as much as it did me. He pauses at the driver's door and makes a subtle adjustment to his trousers, apparently unfazed by the evidence of his arousal. The casual way he handles his body's response only reinforces how different he is from every other man I've known.

The car settles and shifts with his weight as he slides into the driver's seat. The interior feels like sanctuary after the exposure of walking across campus.

"Where are we going?"

"Safe house. Virginia."

"How far?"

"Hour. Maybe ninety minutes with traffic."

An hour trapped in a car with a man who just kissed me senseless as a tactical maneuver. A man whose touch makes me forget every rational thought, whose voice makes me want to obey without question, whose presence makes me feel simultaneously safer and more vulnerable than I've ever been.

This is going to be a very long drive.

"Cooper?"

"Yeah."

"Thank you. For getting me out of there safely."

His eyes meet mine for just a moment. "Job's not done yet."

I should say something about the kiss. The words hover on my tongue, desperate to escape, but what exactly would I say? *Did you feel what I felt back there? Was that real or just tactics? Because I'm pretty sure my knees are still weak from the way you commanded me not to pull away.*

But what if I'm reading too much into it?

What if those kisses were purely professional—just another tool in his tactical arsenal? Except … He was aroused. Unmistakably, obviously aroused.

Men can't fake that kind of physical response, can they?

And the way he looked at my lips afterward, the adjustment he made to his trousers without any embarrassment—that seemed personal, not professional.

Then again, maybe physical arousal doesn't mean anything to a man like Cooper. Maybe it's just biology, a natural response to kissing any attractive woman, regardless of any emotional involvement.

Maybe I'm overthinking this entire situation because I've never experienced anything as intense as his mouth claiming mine.

The silence stretches between us, thick with unspoken questions and the lingering heat of what happened against that car. I want to know what he's thinking, what those kisses meant to him, whether this is just another day at the office or something more. But asking feels too vulnerable, too revealing of how completely he's affected me.

Something fundamental shifted during that kiss, something that goes far beyond professional protection. The question is whether Cooper felt it too, or if I'm reading too much into what was purely a survival tactic.

Whatever this is between us, whatever started in that cold tunnel and exploded during that kiss, it's only going to get more complicated.

And somehow, despite the danger and uncertainty, I'm looking forward to finding out exactly how complicated it can get.

SEVEN

Cooper

COMPLICATIONS

Fuck.

My cock throbs against my zipper as I merge into D.C. traffic, the taste of Dr. Eliza Wren still coating my tongue. Vanilla and heat and something distinctly feminine that makes me want to pull over and finish what that kiss started. The first kiss was a necessity. Phoenix operatives, twelve o'clock, moving past our position. Standard camouflage technique.

The second kiss? Completely unnecessary. Totally on me. I wanted to do it, but I lost sight of the operatives while I was busy claiming her mouth. Stupid from a tactical standpoint, but I couldn't stop myself.

Regardless, mission parameters were satisfied. She's alive.

But her mouth under mine, soft and responsive, those little sounds she made when I commanded her not to pull away—professional distance evaporated like morning dew under direct sunlight.

I want to taste her properly. Take my time. Make her moan again.

God, the way she moaned …

Stupid. Unprofessional. Compromised operational security and client safety.

And now all I can think about is fucking her. Finishing what I started. Taking her clothes off, laying her down, fucking her against the wall, putting her on her knees, fucking her from behind, watching her beg for me as she takes my cock in her mouth. The way she responds to my commands and melts under my authority—it's like crack, and I can't stop thinking about her.

My hand drops to adjust my pants again. Harder than before now, and she notices. Those eyes track the movement before darting away, color flooding her cheeks.

Interesting.

Most women would comment, make jokes, or press the advantage. Dr. Wren sits quietly, fingers twisted in her lap.

She's shy about sex. Academic types usually are—they're all intellectual theory and minimal practical application. Probably spent all of her time in college with her nose buried in a book rather than out at clubs getting fucked in bar bathrooms.

She probably thinks that kiss meant something more than it did, but it was a tactical necessity, even if I ladled on a side of male stupidity.

None of which changes the fact that I'm driving through downtown D.C. with a raging hard-on and a client who smells like vanilla and submission, yet all I can think about is fucking her. Bending her over the hood of this car. Making her scream my name while I pound into her from behind. Watching her come apart under my hands until she can't think, can't speak, can't do anything but take what I give her.

I shake my head hard, forcing my mind back on the mission.

Focus. Professional distance.

Client safety.

Fucking bullshit.

My attention shifts to the rearview mirror—clear. Quick check of the passenger side mirror—clear. Driver's side mirror reveals a black SUV two cars back, government plates visible even at this distance. The same vehicle from campus surveillance yesterday?

Impossible to determine from here, but the way it's maintaining position suggests active pursuit rather than coincidental traffic patterns.

"Who did you see back there? When you kissed me, I mean. Was it the people trying to kill me?"

"Phoenix operatives. Two of them."

"Did they recognize me?"

"No."

"How can you be certain?"

"Because you're still breathing."

She shifts in the passenger seat, and I catch another whiff of that vanilla scent. My cock pulses against my zipper in response, blood flow redirecting from brain to groin when I need tactical clarity most.

Focus. Professional distance. Client safety over personal satisfaction.

"Why did you kiss me?"

The question hangs in the air like cordite after an explosion. Direct. No academic dancing around the subject. She wants answers, but I'm not prepared to give them.

"Tactical camouflage."

"Both times?"

Smart woman. Too fucking smart.

"Situation required—"

My encrypted phone buzzes. Perfect timing. I tap the earpiece, cutting off her question before she can dig deeper into territory that compromises mission parameters.

"Ghost."

"Package secure?" Mason's voice crackles through the connection, steady and professional.

"Affirmative. En route to Virginia safe house."

"ETA?"

Rearview mirror check: black SUV still maintaining position two cars back. The driver is wearing sunglasses despite an overcast morning. Passenger scanning traffic patterns with systematic precision.

"Thirty minutes. Maybe forty with traffic."

"Complications?"

Besides the fact that I'm harder than Chinese arithmetic and fighting the urge to pull over and fuck my client senseless? Besides how she responds to authority, which makes me want to give her orders and watch her body language shift into submission.

"Possible surveillance. Nothing confirmed."

"Need backup?"

"Negative. Situation manageable."

Dr. Wren opens her mouth with another question, but I hold up one finger. Stay quiet. Let me finish the call. She complies immediately, and the automatic obedience sends heat straight to my already aching cock.

Dangerous territory. Client relationships never end well.

"Extraction timeline?" I ask Ghost.

"Seventy-two hours. Maybe ninety-six. Phoenix is adapting faster than anticipated."

"Copy that."

The call ends, and silence fills the car. Dr. Wren sits quietly, hands folded, waiting for permission to speak. The Georgetown sweatshirt I bought off that college student looks a hell of a lot better on her than it did on the original owner—the way it stretches across her chest, highlighting curves that have no business being this distracting during an active protection detail.

Rearview mirror: black SUV has closed the distance. One car

back now, maintaining perfect surveillance interval. Professional work.

"You cut me off," she says finally.

"Important call."

"I was asking important questions."

"No, you were fishing for information."

Color flashes across her cheeks. "I have a right to understand what's happening to me."

"You have a right to stay alive. Everything else is optional."

"That's not—"

"Dr. Wren." Her name comes out sharp enough to cut glass. "Survival trumps curiosity. Every time."

She crosses her arms, which does interesting things to her cleavage. "Don't patronize me."

"Don't ask questions that compromise operational security."

"How does asking why you kissed me compromise operational security?"

Because admitting I want to kiss her again compromises my professional judgment. Because acknowledging this attraction means crossing lines that exist for good reasons. Because explaining that her submission makes me want to do things that have nothing to do with a protection detail opens doors that should stay locked.

"Tactical necessity. End of discussion."

"That's not an answer."

"It's the only answer you're getting."

Passenger side mirror: silver sedan, three cars back, different from the SUV, but maintaining similar surveillance patterns. Two vehicles. Coordinated pursuit. Phoenix has upgraded from single-team operations to multi-vehicle tracking.

Shit.

"You're impossible," she mutters.

"You're alive. That's what matters."

"Is that your solution to everything? Reduce it to survival basics?"

"When people are trying to kill you? Yes."

Driver-side mirror: black SUV has moved up another position. Silver sedan maintaining distance. Professional box formation designed to prevent evasive maneuvers.

This just became significantly more complicated.

"Cooper—"

"Quiet."

My hands tighten on the steering wheel as I process my tactical options. The highway ahead offers limited exit opportunities. The surface streets provide better maneuverability but increased exposure to civilians. The safe house location remains secure, but leading our pursuit directly there compromises any future operations.

I need to lose the tails before proceeding to the extraction point.

"What's wrong?" Dr. Wren's voice carries new tension. Smart enough to read body language changes.

"Possibly nothing."

"That sounds like definitely something."

Rearview mirror: the black SUV is closing distance again. The silver sedan is moving up two lanes over. It's a classic pincer movement in preparation for an intercept. They're not following anymore. They're getting ready to attack or make their move.

My cock finally starts to soften as adrenaline redirects blood flow to more essential systems. About fucking time.

"Buckle your seatbelt."

"It is buckled."

"Tighter."

Her hands move to the belt automatically, adjusting the strap across her chest. The motion draws my attention to her breasts again, and I force my gaze back to the traffic.

Focus. Professional distance. Client safety.

"Cooper, you're scaring me."

"Good. Scared keeps you alive."

Driver-side mirror: the silver sedan is accelerating. The black SUV is matching its speed. They're no longer maintaining surveillance intervals—they're moving into active pursuit configuration.

Two teams. Multiple vehicles. This is a coordinated operation.

Phoenix has definitely upgraded its tactics since Ryan and Celeste's extraction. This isn't random assassination—it's systematic elimination with military precision.

Dr. Eliza Wren just became significantly more valuable than our initial intelligence suggested.

And I just became responsible for keeping her alive against odds that are multiplying by the minute.

Time to see precisely how good Phoenix's new tactical protocols really are.

I take the next exit, merging onto surface streets with aggression. The black SUV follows immediately. The silver sedan takes the exit after, maintaining distance. Professional work, but they're committed now—no more surveillance. They are in full pursuit mode.

"What are you doing?" Dr. Wren grips the door handle as I take a hard right onto M Street.

"Losing them."

"By driving faster?"

"By being unpredictable."

The SUV is two cars back, closing the distance through D.C. traffic. The sedan parallels us one street over—I catch glimpses of it through side streets. They're boxing us in, forcing us toward a predetermined point of interception.

Not happening.

I slam the brakes and take a hard left into a narrow alley behind a row of restaurants. The rental car scrapes brick walls on both sides, but the space is too tight for the SUV to follow. Dr. Wren makes a small sound of alarm as we squeeze through, emerging onto a side street that runs parallel to our original route.

"That was—" she starts.

"Effective."

"Terrifying."

"Same thing."

The rearview mirror shows the alley mouth—no pursuit vehicles in sight, but they'll adapt and redirect, establish new intercept points. Phoenix learns fast. Too fast.

Surface pursuit isn't sustainable. The streets of D.C. offer too many surveillance cameras, too many opportunities for facial recognition software to identify us. Security cameras on every corner, traffic cameras at every intersection, and private security systems feeding data to who knows where. Phoenix can tap into all of it—an AI system with unlimited surveillance access, hunting two people in a car.

The Metro. Underground, there is limited camera coverage and denser crowds to disappear into. There are multiple lines, multiple exit points, and random routing options that even Phoenix can't predict. I'm going to win by being unpredictable.

By being human.

I need to ditch the car.

"Where are we going?" Dr. Wren asks as I turn onto Connecticut Avenue.

"Metro."

"We're taking the subway?"

"Unless you prefer being shot."

"That's not—why can't we just drive to wherever we're going?"

"Because they're tracking the car."

"How do you know that?"

"Because that's what I would do."

I don't know how they're tracking the car. I was pretty damn sure about getting her out of there clean—no one was following us when we left campus. But somehow Phoenix identified her, and now they've identified me. They can track license plates through traffic cameras and facial recognition through surveillance networks. I've got to get rid of the car, but there are cameras everywhere.

I pull into a parking garage three blocks from Dupont Circle station. Not ideal—security cameras at the entrance—but better than street parking. The rental car goes on level three, tucked between a van and an SUV that provides visual screening.

"Out. Move fast."

Dr. Wren fumbles with her seatbelt, and I reach across to release it myself. The contact puts my hand inches from her thigh, and the vanilla scent hits me again. Focus. Professional distance.

"Cooper, I need to know—"

"Talk while walking."

I grab her hand and pull her toward the garage exit. Her fingers are soft, warm, smaller than mine in a way that makes something protective flare in my chest. I like the feel of her hand in mine.

It feels normal, walking with her, holding her hand. I don't do this with any other protection details, but I'm doing it with her, and I don't know what that means. But it can't be good.

Dangerous territory.

The street level bustles with typical D.C. foot traffic—tourists, business people, students. Perfect cover, except for the surveillance cameras mounted on every corner. I keep Dr. Wren close, her body shielding part of my profile from overhead angles.

"Where exactly are we going?" she asks, slightly breathless from keeping up with my pace.

"Safe house."

"You said that before. Where is this safe house?"

"Secure location."

"That's not an answer."

"It's the only answer you're getting."

EIGHT

Cooper

UNDERGROUND

A CONVENIENCE STORE APPEARS ON THE CORNER AHEAD, THE KIND of place that sells everything from magazines to basic clothing. Perfect.

"In here," I say, pulling her toward the entrance.

"Why are we stopping?"

"Clothing change."

"What's wrong with what we're wearing?"

"They're tracking our appearance."

Inside, I grab an armload of items—three different T-shirts for her, three for me, a baseball cap, and new sunglasses. The clerk barely looks up from his phone as I dump cash on the counter.

"Bathroom," I tell Dr. Wren, handing her the shirts. "Change into one of these. Keep the jeans and shoes."

"Which one?"

"Doesn't matter. Just different."

While she disappears into the small bathroom, I pull on a plain black T-shirt over my tactical vest, switching out my jacket for a navy hoodie from the rack. The baseball cap sits low over my eyes, and the new sunglasses complete the transformation.

When she emerges wearing a bright blue T-shirt that makes her eyes stand out even more, I hand her the remaining clothes.

"Carry these. We'll change again later."

"This is insane."

"This is survival."

The Dupont Circle Metro entrance appears ahead—concrete steps leading down into D.C.'s underground transit system. Red line, blue line, orange line—multiple options for routing, multiple opportunities to lose pursuit through random direction changes.

"I've never taken the Metro," Dr. Wren says as we approach the entrance.

I stop walking and stare at her. "You've never taken the Metro? You live in D.C. Everyone takes the Metro."

"I live in a brownstone near Georgetown. I walk when I can, drive when I need to. I like being outside, not underground in crowds and tunnels."

I shake my head. "That's weird."

"It's not weird, it's a preference."

"First time for everything."

"What if I don't know how to—"

"Follow my lead. Stay close. Do what I say when I say it."

The steps descend into the familiar underground world of D.C.'s subway system. Tile walls stretch in long corridors, fluorescent lighting casting everything in harsh white. The smell hits immediately—recycled air, cleaning chemicals, the faint odor of too many people in enclosed spaces.

Dr. Wren's hand tightens in mine as we navigate the corridors. Smart woman—underground spaces feel different when people are hunting you. More confined. Limited escape routes.

"How do you know which train to take?" she asks.

"I don't."

"What do you mean you don't know?"

"Random routing. Harder to predict."

The platform opens up before us—two tracks, multiple destinations. Orange line toward Vienna, blue line toward Franconia. I scan the electronic displays, calculating timing and crowd density.

The orange line arrives first. There is a moderate crowd, enough people to provide cover without creating mobility problems. I make the random choice and we head that way.

"This one," I say, guiding her toward the train doors.

We board with the usual rush of commuters. I position Dr. Wren against the far wall and stand facing her, my body creating a visual barrier between her and the other passengers. The position puts her pressed against my chest, and I can feel every breath she takes.

"Why are you standing so close?" she whispers.

"Surveillance screening."

"This feels like—"

"Like, what?"

Color floods her cheeks. "Nothing."

I lean in and whisper in her ear. "Sorry, love. You only get the kisses when people are actually trying to find us."

She jerks back from me, eyes wide. "That's not what I was going to say."

"No, but you were thinking it."

"How do you know?"

"Because I was thinking exactly the same thing."

The train pulls away from the platform, and I scan the other passengers. Business suits, tourists with cameras, and a few college students. No obvious threats, but Phoenix operatives blend in. Professional training teaches them to look like everyone else.

I love the pink flush of her cheeks, the way I flustered her. So flustered, in fact, that her nonstop verbal dialogue has completely stopped. I made her speechless, and I fucking love that.

My arm slides around her lower back, pulling her closer against me.

"What are you doing?" she whispers.

"Just because I'm not kissing you doesn't mean we can't look like a couple riding the train. We're going for camouflage."

"Cooper, about what happened earlier—"

"Not now."

"When you kissed me—"

I lean in close to her ear. "Eliza. That was an order. What do you do with my orders?"

"Obey them," she responds, sarcasm dripping from her voice.

"That's right. You obey my orders. You do as I say. Our number one priority is staying alive. Everything else takes a backseat to that. If I need to hold you close, I'm gonna hold you close. If I need to kiss you, I'm gonna kiss you. I'm gonna do whatever the hell it takes to keep you alive."

Her eyes widen at my unusually long speech. "Wow. If I knew that talking about that kiss would make you say more than one or two words, I would've done it earlier."

She opens her mouth with another question, but the train slows for the next station. Rosslyn. I evaluate the platform through the windows—normal foot traffic, no obvious surveillance.

"We're getting off," I announce.

"But we just got on."

"Random routing, remember?"

I take her hand again and guide her through the doors onto the Rosslyn platform. The train pulls away, carrying our previous location into the tunnel. Anyone tracking our movement has lost the trail.

The blue line platform. It's a different direction with different destinations. The crowd here is thinner. It's late morning weekend traffic rather than rush hour chaos. Perfect time to change our clothes.

"This way." I steer her toward the restrooms.

"What are we doing?"

"Clothing change number two."

I guide her past the separate men's and women's restrooms to the family restroom at the end of the corridor. Single occupancy, lockable door, private space.

"What the hell are we doing in here?" she asks as I shut the door behind us and engage the lock.

"Changing clothes."

I pull out one of the other shirts from the convenience store and strip off the black T-shirt, replacing it with a gray one. When I turn around, she's standing frozen by the door, clutching her bag of clothes.

"I'm not going to change with you looking at me."

"Look, I can stare at the door, I can stare at the mirror, I can look at you—whatever you want. Change your shirt and let's get going. We don't have time to argue."

She starts removing the blue T-shirt from the convenience store, then pauses. "You know, it's kind of a shame about all these clothes. That Georgetown hoodie—I would've liked to have kept it. You spent $200 on it."

"Technically, it was $200 for everything. Anyway, it's gone."

"Now what do I do with this shirt?"

"Put it in the trash."

She looks at me and rolls her eyes like that makes no sense at all. Then she starts to shrug the other shirt over her sweater.

"You're gonna ditch the sweater too."

"Why do I need to ditch the sweater?"

"Because it changes your silhouette. Everything comes off but the new shirt."

When she pauses, I add, "Eliza. That was an order."

She rolls her eyes. "Fine. But you need to turn around."

I turn toward the mirror, and she pulls off her sweater. The reflection gives me a perfect view of her delicate lace bra barely containing those voluptuous tits that have been driving me crazy all morning. My mind goes straight back into the gutter.

Shit. I should've just stared at the wall.

"Fine. I'm done. Now what?"

"Give me the shirt you took off."

She hands me the blue T-shirt, and I lead her out of the bathroom, stuffing both shirts into the nearest waste receptacle.

"This is making me dizzy," Dr. Wren says as we wait for the next train.

"Good. Means it's working."

"How do you know where we're going?"

"I don't."

"That's impossible. You have to have a plan."

"The plan is *unpredictability*."

"That's not a plan, that's chaos."

"Sometimes chaos is the best plan."

The blue line train arrives, and we board again. This time, I position us in the middle of the car, surrounded by other passengers on all sides. Dr. Wren ends up pressed even closer against me, her breasts against my chest, her face tilted up toward mine.

The position sends heat racing through my system again. Wrong time, wrong place, but my body doesn't care about tactical considerations when she's looking at me with those green eyes.

"Cooper," she says quietly, "I need to understand what's happening between us."

"Nothing's happening."

A whole lot is happening. I'm just not going to admit it to her.

"That's not true."

"It's tactical necessity." And I'm trying to convince myself as much as her. "I'm saving your life. That's what's happening."

"That's not true. There's more—"

"Like what? More what?"

"The kiss. Both kisses."

"Don't try to overthink it."

She stops walking and stares at me. "I'm not an idiot. I'm a linguist, and one of the things linguists do is study behavior. It's not about the words—it's about the behavior. Something is happening here, and I want to know what it is."

"Why do you need to know? Why do you need to analyze it? It was a kiss. Just leave it at that. Come on, let's go."

The lie comes out easily, but her expression suggests she doesn't believe it. Smart woman. Too fucking smart.

"You're lying."

"I'm protecting you."

"By lying to me?"

"By keeping you focused on survival instead of—"

"Instead of what?"

Instead of the way you respond to my commands. Instead of how your body melts against mine when I take control. Instead of the fact that I want to drag you into the nearest dark corner and finish what that kiss started.

"Instead of complications."

The train slows for Metro Center. Major hub station, multiple lines, crowds. Perfect location for another direction change.

"Off," I say, taking her hand.

"Again?"

"Again."

Metro Center's platform spreads out in multiple directions—red line, orange line, and blue line connections. The crowd here is thick, with constant movement in all directions. Exactly what we need.

I guide Dr. Wren through the crowd toward the red line platform. She keeps pace without complaint, but the questions continue.

"How long are we going to keep riding trains in circles?"

"Until I'm satisfied we're clean."

"Clean of what?"

"Surveillance."

"How will you know?"

"Experience."

"That's not an answer."

"It's the only answer you're getting."

The red line train arrives, packed with passengers. Perfect. I push Dr. Wren ahead of me, then position myself behind her, my chest against her back, my arms bracketing her against the train wall.

The position is intimate, possessive, and completely necessary for security. At least that's what I tell myself.

"Cooper," she says quietly, her voice barely audible over the train noise.

"Yeah."

"This feels like more than tactical positioning."

My jaw clenches. She's right, and we both know it. But acknowledging that truth leads down paths that compromise mission parameters.

"It's whatever it needs to be to keep you alive."

"And after? When I'm safe?"

After. When the mission ends and she returns to her academic life? I'll disappear back into the shadows.

"There is no after."

The words come out harsher than intended, but they're true. Protection details end. Clients return to their everyday lives. Operators move on to the next mission.

Except the way she feels pressed against me suggests this mission might be different.

The train pulls into Union Station. Major terminus, multiple exit routes, crowds thick enough to disappear into.

"This is us," I say.

We exit with the mass of commuters, and I keep Dr. Wren close as we navigate the station's main concourse. Union Station bustles with travelers, tourists, and locals—perfect cover for the final approach to the safe house.

"Where now?" she asks as we emerge onto street level.

"Walking distance."

"How far?"

"Six blocks."

The safe house sits in a residential neighborhood north of Union Station—a nondescript row house that looks exactly like every other row house on the block. Perfect camouflage in plain sight.

I scan the street as we approach, looking for surveillance, out-of-place vehicles, anything that suggests Phoenix has anticipated our destination. Everything appears normal—parked cars, pedestrians, the usual rhythm of urban residential life.

"This is it," I say, guiding her up the front steps.

The lock disengages with my key card, and we step into the safe house's interior. Basic furnishings, secure communications equipment, and a weapons cache in the basement. Everything needed for extended protection operations.

"We made it," Dr. Wren says, relief evident in her voice.

"Yeah. We made it."

But as I engage the electronic locks and activate the security system, something in my gut suggests this is far from over. Phoenix doesn't give up easily, and Dr. Eliza Wren represents something valuable enough to justify escalating tactics.

The question is what happens when Phoenix decides that ground pursuit isn't sufficient.

And whether this safe house is actually safe at all.

NINE

Eliza

BREAKING POINT

THE SAFE HOUSE DOOR CLICKS SHUT BEHIND US WITH A FINALITY
that makes my pulse jump. Cooper engages multiple locks—electronic, mechanical, and a security system that beeps as it
activates.

We're sealed in. Trapped. Together.

Seventy-two hours of nowhere to run. Maybe longer.

No distractions. No escape. Just him and me.

"This is impressive." My voice is pitched higher than usual,
nerves vibrating through every syllable. "The security measures, I
mean. How many different lock systems are there? And the location—residential neighborhood, completely nondescript. Perfect
camouflage. No one would suspect this is anything other than a
normal row house. The architectural details are authentic too.
Did Cerberus design this, or did you acquire an existing property
and retrofit it?"

Cooper moves through the space with lethal calm, checking
the windows and scanning the street through gaps in the blinds.

Silent. Controlled. Dangerous.

He doesn't answer.

Which only makes me talk faster.

"The furniture looks deliberately generic. Practical but forgettable. Nothing that would stand out in anyone's memory. And these walls—are they reinforced? They appear to be thicker than standard residential construction. Probably bulletproof, right? How long has this location been operational? Do you have multiple safe houses, or is this the primary—"

"For the love of God," Cooper cuts me off, voice like sandpaper and heat, turning to face me with an expression I can't quite decode.

His green eyes are locked on me—intense, unblinking, loaded with a tension that has nothing to do with logistics and everything to do with us.

The space between us tightens.

"Do you ever shut up?"

The words should land like an insult. But they don't.

Not with that look in his eyes.

That predatory stillness. That heat curling behind his gaze, restrained by the thinnest thread.

My breath catches.

"No," I say, chin tipping up. "I don't. I process verbally. It's how my brain works. If that bothers you—"

I don't get to finish.

He closes the space between us in two brutal strides, hands framing my face, body pinning mine against the wall.

His mouth crashes down on mine with no finesse, no permission, no hesitation.

Just hunger.

Wild. Unleashed. Consuming.

My hands fist in his shirt, clinging, pulling him closer as his tongue claims my mouth—deep, possessive, absolute.

Something I'll never recover from.

He pulls back enough to look at me, his breathing ragged, jaw clenched like he's on the edge of losing control.

"There." His voice is raw. Rough. Dangerous. "Finally found a way to shut you up."

My cheeks burn—not with embarrassment, but from the way he's staring at me.

Like I'm something he wants to break open and devour.

Fire licks through me. My core clenches.

"Cooper," I whisper, but I don't even know what I'm trying to say. Every synapse has gone offline, short-circuited by the way he tastes, the way he feels, the weight of him between me and the wall.

"I'm going to fuck you now," he says, and the words hit like a blow. "Put that mouth to better use."

A pause. His gaze flicks over my face, daring me to stop him.

"You've got one chance to say no. One. But if you don't, the same rules apply."

My breath catches. "What rules?"

"I give the orders," he says, voice dark and absolute. "And you obey."

The world tilts. Heat floods me, sharp and dizzying.

This is it.

The fantasy I've never spoken aloud.

The one with leather and iron and blood-soaked sand.

A warrior strong enough to take.

A man who commands.

"Are you always this bossy?" I whisper, trying to breathe past the knot in my throat.

His mouth curls into a feral smile. "If you thought I was bossy before, you have no idea what I'm like when I fuck."

The words melt through me like lava. My knees weaken. My pulse slams behind my ribs.

He braces one palm against the wall beside my head, leaning in until his breath ghosts over my ear.

"Last chance, Eliza."

I shake my head. Quick. Shallow.

I'm not stopping this.

Not now. Not when he's touched a part of me no one else ever has.

Something fierce flashes in his eyes—dark, possessive, hungry.

Without a word, he grabs my waist and lifts me like I weigh nothing, pinning me to the wall, my feet dangling, helpless.

The display of strength, the sheer ease with which he moves me exactly where he wants me, lights a fire in my blood.

This is the fantasy. Not soft. Not sweet. Just raw, undeniable power.

He crashes his mouth onto mine again, and this time I don't just lose myself—I give in. Completely.

His hands are everywhere—buried in my hair, gripping my hips, flattening me against the wall like he's marking territory. I feel every line of him—every hard muscle, every taut inch—his cock pressed thick and unmistakable against my belly.

When his mouth drags to my neck, my body arches into him. A soft moan escapes—high, desperate, unguarded.

The sound snaps something in him.

He growls against my skin and lifts me higher, my legs wrapping around his waist. The hard jut of him grinds between my thighs, right where I need it.

"Bedroom or here?" His voice is a rasp against my throat. "Your choice. Last one you'll get tonight."

My breath stutters. "Is that possible?"

His mouth curves into a wicked smile, teeth flashing like a predator who's already caught his prey.

"Darling," he murmurs, "you have no idea how I love to fuck."

The vulgar promise paired with the casual endearment makes my whole body clench.

"Bedroom," I whisper, barely able to form the word.

He doesn't hesitate.

He carries me down the hallway like I weigh nothing, heat radiating off him in waves. At the door, he doesn't fumble or pause—he shoulders it open and deposits me on the bed like he's staking a claim.

The room is bland. Generic.

But Cooper?

He looks like every dangerous, filthy, forbidden dream I've ever had.

His tactical vest hits the floor, followed by his shirt.

My breath catches.

He's all rough-cut muscle and hard-earned scars. Strength without vanity. Power without apology.

When he reaches for the hem of my shirt, I raise my arms, trembling.

His eyes burn as he peels the fabric away. "I've thought about these," he says, rough and low, cupping my breasts through the lace. "Every time you talked. Every time you wouldn't shut up."

He squeezes, slow and deliberate, thumbs teasing my nipples until I gasp.

"That," he says, "right there. I'll drag that sound out of you a thousand ways."

His hands move to the clasp of my bra. One flick. It falls away.

Something small hits the floor with a soft clink.

The flash drive.

We both freeze, staring at the tiny piece of metal that started this nightmare.

Cooper moves like he might bend for it—but I catch his arm.

"Cooper," I say, breathless, desperate. "It can wait. Please—I need you."

His low chuckle vibrates through his chest. "Needy, much?"

I flush, but I don't flinch. "Yes."

That one word makes his eyes go molten.

"One thing you need to learn, Eliza …" He steps closer, gaze locked on mine. "I'm in charge here. You don't set the pace."

He lets the flash drive lie forgotten and turns his full attention back to me—like I'm the only mission that matters now.

"But since you asked so nicely …" He lowers his mouth to my ear. "Tell me what you want."

"I want you," I whisper. "All of you."

He doesn't need anything more.

His hands make quick work of the rest of my clothes, his mouth following the path down my skin like he's memorizing me with his tongue.

When he pushes me onto the bed and settles between my thighs, I forget how to think—how to breathe.

"Look at me," he commands.

My eyes snap open, locking on his.

"I want to watch you come apart."

The authority in his voice sends lightning straight through my core.

He leans in, his mouth finding the sweet spot where my neck meets my shoulder—and bites.

I cry out, my hands fisting in the sheets as my hips buck toward him.

"That's it," he growls against my skin. "Let me hear you."

TEN

Eliza

SURRENDER

Everything that follows is heat.

No—fire.

It rolls over me in waves, sensation after sensation crashing so fast I can't keep up.

Cooper doesn't touch—he consumes.

His hands roam like he owns me, like he's been waiting to tear me apart and finally has permission. His mouth is everywhere—sucking, biting, claiming. Down my throat. Across my breasts.

Lower still.

When he drags his tongue between my thighs and groans like I'm his favorite goddamn meal, my legs shake so hard I nearly sob.

"You're dripping," he mutters, voice rough as gravel, eyes blazing between my legs. "Fuck, look at this sweet little pussy. You soaked the sheets for me, baby."

I can't answer. Can't speak. Just moan as he slides two fingers inside me, slow and deliberate, then curls them just right.

"Arch for me," he growls. "I want that greedy cunt to grind against my face."

And I do.

I can't not.

He devours me like a man starved—using his fingers, his tongue, his voice, dragging me up to the edge again and again until I'm pleading, my thighs shaking around his head, my voice wrecked.

"Come on my tongue," he snarls. "Give it to me, Eliza. Right fucking now."

I shatter.

Hard.

My cry rips through the room, sharp and desperate and real. My body jerks off the bed, everything tightening around his mouth, his hand, him.

He doesn't stop. Doesn't let me float away.

Just kisses my inner thigh, then slides up my body in one lethal, fluid movement—lining himself up, pressing the thick head of his cock against my entrance.

"Look at me."

My eyes snap open, locking on his.

"You ready for this?"

I nod.

He doesn't move.

"Use your words, baby. I want to hear it."

"Yes," I gasp.

He thrusts in one brutal, perfect stroke that forces the air from my lungs.

I scream.

The stretch, the fullness—it's too much and not enough all at once.

"Goddamn," he growls. "Tight little hole taking every fucking inch."

He holds still, breathing hard.

"Okay?" he asks, voice strained. Barely controlled.

"More than okay," I whisper. "Don't stop. Please don't stop."

"Not a chance in hell," he growls.

He starts to move.

Not fast—not yet.

Each thrust is measured, claiming. Deep enough to bruise. Slow enough to torment.

His hands grip my hips, controlling every angle. His mouth drags down my jaw, biting my shoulder.

"Fucking made for me," he pants. "You feel that? That's me splitting you open. Filling every goddamn inch."

I whimper, my nails digging into his back.

"You love this," he growls. "Being fucked the way you need."

"Yes," I sob, already trembling. "Yes—Cooper, please—"

"That's it," he rasps, speeding up now. "Beg for it. Beg for your fucking release."

"Please," I moan. "Please—I need to come—"

"You don't need anything unless I say so."

He grabs my wrists, pins them above my head.

"You come when I let you. Not before."

His other hand slips between us, thumb circling my clit in perfect, torturous rhythm.

"You'll take what I give," he growls. "Every thrust. Every command. Every filthy fucking word."

My body is a live wire—every nerve lit, strung so tight I'm seconds from detonation.

"I want to watch you fall apart," he whispers, mouth at my ear. "I want to fuck you so hard you can't remember your own goddamn name."

He drives in—harder now—deep, fast, relentless.

The slap of skin-on-skin echoes in the room, punctuated by my moans, my cries, the rough curses falling from his lips.

"That's my girl," he snarls as I start to break. "Take what you fucking need."

It hits me like a detonation.

My back bows off the bed, my body convulsing around him, eyes wide open as I scream his name and come harder than I ever have in my life.

Cooper doesn't slow.

He fucks me through it.

"I'm not done," he groans. "Not until I'm buried so deep you forget you were ever anyone else's."

Another thrust. Another.

He slams in once more and growls against my throat as he comes—hard—his cock pulsing inside me, his voice breaking on my name like a goddamn prayer.

He collapses on top of me, panting, sweaty, shaking.

I feel wrecked. Stretched. Claimed.

Exactly how I wanted to feel.

Exactly how he promised I would.

Afterward, we lie tangled together, limbs a mess, skin slick with sweat, still gasping.

My body feels wrecked in the best way—every nerve raw, overstimulated, alive.

His arm is heavy across my waist. His breath brushes the crown of my head.

My academic brain tries to reassert itself, clinging to routine —to logic—but it short-circuits the moment I try to analyze what happened. There's no category for this. No metric.

This wasn't sex.

It was a seismic event.

"Well," I say, breathless, my voice barely more than a whisper. "That's one way to shut me up."

Cooper's chest rumbles with a quiet, satisfied laugh. "Most effective method I've found so far."

I roll onto my side, propping myself up on one elbow. He looks different like this—less contained. Hair mussed. Eyes softened. Smug, yes, but also something else.

Relaxed.

Real.

"Cooper," I start.

But he lifts a hand and places two fingers against my lips.

"Don't overthink it," he says.

I nod, but my brain's already spinning. Part of me needs to ask what this means. If it's just sex, or if it could be anything else.

But another part of me—the part still humming with orgasmic aftershocks—is content to stay here in his arms. Let the questions wait.

For now, we're safe.

Not just physically. Emotionally.

Outside, Phoenix is still hunting. Our reality still waits with teeth bared.

But right here, right now, I feel protected in a way no perimeter check or reinforced wall could ever match.

"Seventy-two hours," I murmur into his chest.

"Maybe ninety-six," he corrects, tightening his grip like he's claiming every second.

"Good," I say, and I mean it with everything I've got left.

"Why's that good?"

"Because that gives you more time to show me all those tactical positions."

His laugh vibrates against my skin. "Is that what we're calling it?"

"What else would you call it?"

"Hot sex." He grins. "But if you think I'm good for only one round, you've got another thing coming."

I blink. The words trip something automatic in my brain.

"Technically," I murmur, still breathless, "it's 'another think coming.' It's a misheard idiom—an eggcorn. The original phrase — 'If you think that, you've got another think coming' dates back to the early 1900s, not 'thing.' Though the modern misusage has gained—"

His gaze sharpens. Slow. Lethal.

"Eliza." His voice is low. Rough. Laced with danger. "If you don't shut that pretty little mouth right now, I'm going to shove my cock in it and fuck you silent."

The words slice through the air like a blade.

I freeze.

My mouth stops mid-syllable. My brain, always racing, skids and crashes.

Did he just—

"Jesus," he mutters, eyes locked on mine. "You like that, don't you?"

I stare at him, speechless. My skin flushes, my thighs instinctively clenching.

"Yeah," he breathes, dark delight flickering in his eyes. "You're looking at me like I just ripped the thought right out of your dirtiest little fantasy."

I go completely still. Just stare at him. Mortified.

He shifts, rolling me flat, moving over me, still hard, still hungry.

"You gonna play innocent now?" he growls, sliding a hand between my thighs. "After coming all over my cock like that? After crying out my name like you were begging me to ruin you again?"

His fingers find me—slick, throbbing. I jolt.

"You think I don't know what's going on in that brilliant little brain of yours?" He leans in, lips brushing my ear. "You want it. Not the dirty talk. Not the dominance." He drags his fingers over my clit—slow. Unforgiving. "You want to be taken. To be on your knees, choking on my cock."

My breath catches.

He sees it.

Heat flares like I've been struck by a live wire.

His eyes narrow with the satisfaction of a man who just detonated a charge and liked the explosion. "Yeah, that turns you the fuck on," he murmurs, moving in closer. "I hit on one of your filthy little fantasies."

I try to speak, but nothing comes out. Not a single word.

"Now that's a first," he growls. "Professor Motor Mouth, rendered speechless by the thought of choking on my cock."

God.

He's in my head.

He's inside the fantasy I've never said out loud.

The Roman gladiator. The conqueror. The brute who doesn't ask—he takes. Puts me on my knees and feeds me every inch of him because he can. Because I want him to.

Cooper brushes my hair off my face with an almost gentle touch. But his next words are anything but soft.

"If you thought round one was the end of it, sweetheart—" his voice drops, dark and rough, "—you've got something else to think about. I'm not done. I'm going to tear you apart. Ruin you. Again. And again. You're going to come on my face, on my cock, on my fingers. Until you can't even remember how to form a single goddamn word."

He kisses me, but it's not a kiss.

It's a claim. All tongue and hunger, heat and control.

When he finally pulls back, his breath fans hot against my lips. "And when you're finally spent—when you're limp and wrecked and twitching—I want you to look me in the eye and tell me exactly what went through that brilliant little linguist brain of yours when I told you I was going to fuck your mouth."

His fingers slide between my thighs, and I jerk at the sudden jolt of pleasure. He chuckles darkly as his fingers begin to move.

It's not gentle. It's not teasing. It's pressure—blunt, precise, claiming.

My hips buck instinctively, breath catching hard in my chest.

He watches me. Silent. Sharp. That infuriatingly smug grin tugging at the corner of his mouth.

"Yeah," he murmurs. "Speechless again."

His fingers work deeper, parting me. Finding exactly where I need him and pressing, stroking, pushing me toward the edge like he owns my body.

Like he already knows how it breaks.

My spine bows off the bed. Hands scrabble for something—anything—to hold on to.

I can't. I can't stop it. It's too much. Too fast.

My thighs tremble, clenching around his wrist as a sob of pleasure rips from my throat.

"That's it," he growls, fingers relentless. "Come for me. Soak my hand, Eliza."

And I do.

Hard.

Shaking.

Lips parted around a sound I don't even recognize as my own.

Before I can recover, he grabs my hips. Flips me onto my stomach like I weigh nothing.

My cheek hits the mattress. A heartbeat later—

CRACK.

His hand lands on my ass, sharp and commanding. The sting ricochets through me, raw and electric.

I gasp, heat blooming across my skin.

"Good girl," he growls, voice dark with satisfaction. "But we're not done."

His palm presses between my shoulder blades. Heavy. Possessive. Controlling.

I go still. Breath caught.

"My turn." He kneels behind me, shoves my thighs wide, and drags the thick head of his cock through my slick folds—slow, deliberate, filthy.

No warning.

He drives into me in one rough, ruthless thrust.

I cry out—more shock than pain—my hands fisting the sheets as he fills me completely.

His hand curls into my hair, yanks me back just enough to bare my throat.

"Looks like my little linguist likes it rough." His breath is hot at my ear. "Feel it. Feel me fucking you. Taking you. Using you. Until you can't fucking walk."

He thrusts again—hard. Deep. Right into the spot that makes me see stars.

And again.

And again.

Relentless.

Claiming.

Exactly the way I always imagined it would feel to be taken by a man who doesn't ask—who just knows.

The sound of skin slapping skin, the sting of his hand tangled in my hair, the obscene stretch of him inside me—it's all too much.

Too perfect.

My vision blurs as I shatter again, my body convulsing around him, his name tearing from my throat.

Cooper follows with a broken growl, grinding into me as he comes, his hand fisted in my hair, his body locked tight against mine.

We collapse in a tangle of limbs, gasping. Spent. Ruined.

And still—I know round three is coming.

Because the man behind me hasn't begun to be done.

ELEVEN

Eliza

REVEALED

My body's still twitching, face down on the mattress, when he pulls out—slow and deliberate. The kind of drag that leaves me gasping into the sheets, half-wrecked, half-waiting.

I don't move. Can't. Muscles gone soft and shaky.

But he doesn't stop.

He doesn't let me drift off into that satisfied haze. Doesn't even let me breathe it in.

Rough hands flip me again, fast—like I'm nothing but weight he owns, flesh he earned.

His body cages mine. Eyes sharp. Still hard.

Still ready.

"Thought that was the end?" His voice is low, ragged. "Nah, sweetheart. We're not done."

He settles between my thighs again, cock brushing my slick folds—not pushing in.

Teasing.

Threatening.

I moan, hips arching.

He doesn't give me what I need.

Instead, his hand slides low. One thick finger circling my clit with maddening precision. Just enough pressure to light the fuse.

"You're gonna tell me, Eliza."

His mouth is at my throat. Tongue tasting sweat, sex and, shame.

"Tell you what?" I pant, even though I know.

I know.

"You know what," he murmurs. "That look you gave me—when I said I'd shut you up with my cock. Your eyes blew wide and your cunt went soaking wet."

He strokes me again. A slick, deliberate circle that makes my breath catch.

"You've fantasized about it," he growls, biting down just below my ear. "Haven't you?"

I stay silent.

He slides lower. One finger. Two. Deep.

A thrust that makes my back arch and my legs shake. Then he pulls out. Stops.

No rhythm. No friction. Just the unbearable edge of it.

"You did, didn't you?" he murmurs, dragging his tongue down my jaw. "All that brainpower. All that goddamn education. And your biggest fantasy is getting fucked like a mouthy little whore."

"Cooper—"

He thrusts again, deeper this time. Then stops.

I choke on a sound. My hips rock up, seeking more, desperate.

He denies me again.

"This is how this works," he says, voice like gravel and sin. "You tell me the truth, or I don't let you come."

Another thrust. Slow. Cruel.

"You hold out on me, I keep edging you till you're crying."

His fingers slide out. I make a noise—frustration, pain, heat.

"Fuck, you're dripping for it," he murmurs, sliding his thumb over my clit. "So greedy. But you don't get shit until you confess."

"Confess, what?" I whisper, already shaking.

His laugh is dark. Rough. "You know what."

He moves back, positioning himself at my entrance. Not entering. Just resting there.

The pressure is maddening.

"I'm gonna fuck you slow," he says, voice sharp with control. "Real slow. And I'm gonna stop every single time you get close. Until you break."

He pushes in. Agonizingly slow.

One inch.

Two.

Three.

I cry out, nails digging into the sheets.

Then he pulls out completely.

"Tell me," he grits.

I shake my head. I can't. It's too much. Too real.

He sinks in again, faster this time. And pulls out again.

The sound I make isn't human.

My body begs.

My mouth stays shut.

He leans in, breath hot on my lips. "I want to hear it, Eliza. The fantasy. The one you never told anyone. What did you imagine?"

His thumb circles my clit again. Just enough.

"Getting face-fucked by some brute? No mercy, no softness, just his cock down your throat because you talked too much?"

I sob.

But I don't answer.

He stills, buried just barely inside me. His breath brushes my ear.

"I'm right, aren't I. You and your filthy fantasies? You fantasized about being a whore?" he says—testing. "Getting used like one?"

I go quiet.

Too quiet.

He catches it.

His tone shifts.

"No," he mutters, more to himself now. "Not a whore. They get to choose."

His cock slips deeper, painfully slow.

"Ah, I know." He pauses, a smirk on his face. "You don't want to choose. You want to be claimed."

How does he know?

He pulls back. Thrusts hard enough to knock the air from my lungs.

"You fantasize about being a slave, don't you?"

My eyes squeeze shut.

My body clenches around him in answer.

He groans—guttural, wrecked.

"Jesus. That's it."

Another thrust. Deeper. Rougher.

"You want to be the prize," he snarls. "The spoils of war. Dragged in chains to the champion's bed."

I sob out something that's almost his name.

He moves faster now, cock driving into me with brutal certainty.

"You want him to take your mouth. To fuck it until you can't breathe. Until you forget you ever had a name."

His hand fists in my hair, yanks my head back as he slams in again. "Say it."

"No." The word is tiny. Defiant. Fragile.

He stills inside me.

"Oh, Eliza ..." His voice is molten steel, low and lethal. "That's not how this works."

He pulls back slow. Drags out every inch.

"I command. You obey."

Another thrust—deep and sharp. I gasp.

"Now tell me." His mouth is at my ear, breath hot, filthy. "Admit your deepest, darkest fantasy to me."

I shake my head.

Tears sting my eyes. My teeth sink into my bottom lip so hard I taste blood.

Shame burns up my spine like wildfire.

I can't.

He pushes deeper, then stops. Holds.

His fingers press harder into my hip. Unforgiving. Unrelenting.

"You think I don't feel it?" he growls. "The way your pussy clamps down every time I mention being used? That's not fear, Eliza. It's desire. Need. It's fucking raw and honest, and hot as sin."

A broken sound tears from my throat.

"Give it to me," he says, dragging out with brutal slowness. "Or I'll keep you here on the edge all fucking night."

Another thrust. Just enough to threaten my sanity.

"I'll ruin your mind before I let you come again."

My body trembles. My breath shudders out.

He waits.

Cock buried deep.

Breath ragged against my skin.

"Tell me what you want." His command comes hard, cutting through the last of my resistance.

I break.

"Fine," I gasp. "I want to be his slave."

He doesn't move.

Doesn't breathe.

Then—he growls.

Low. Filthy. Animal. Primitive.

It rips out of him like instinct.

His mouth finds the shell of my ear, his voice a dark whisper soaked in sin.

"You want to know my filthiest, most secret, darkest fantasy?"

I don't answer.

I don't have to.

"I want to be the fucking conqueror," he breathes. "The one who wins the war. Who fucks his slaves. Takes them whenever, however, and as many times as he wants."

He thrusts deep, slow, grinding into me like he's driving the words home.

"And I don't know who the hell he is, the one you were fantasizing about all these years …" His hand fists in my hair, yanking my head back just enough for his voice to hit bare skin. "… but you belong to me now."

A dark, satisfied chuckle vibrates against my neck.

Hot breath. Pure claim.

"Looks like we were made for each other, sweetheart."

He starts to move. Hard. Relentless. Each thrust a brand.

"I'm going to ruin you, Eliza," he growls. "Ruin you so fucking deep you'll forget what freedom ever felt like."

He drives in again, brutal and raw, then leans closer, his voice a whip across my spine.

"How does it feel?"

Another thrust.

"To know you're mine."

Another.

"To know you're just a tight, dripping little prize I get to use whenever I want."

I cry out. Not from pain.

From the overwhelming, brutal truth of it.

His hand wraps around my throat—not squeezing. Claiming.

His cock buried to the hilt.

"Say it," he snarls. "Say you're mine."

And I do.

My body splinters around him. Heat crashing through me like fire on dry timber.

"Please," I sob. "Please—more—please—"

"Come," he demands. "Now."

Helpless. Violent. Loud.

My orgasm rips through me like lightning—hot, devastating, complete.

He doesn't stop. Doesn't let me breathe.

He fucks me through the tremors until he finds his own edge—buries himself to the hilt with a broken, wrecked groan.

When he comes, it feels like a claim.

His weight sinks onto me. His breath ghosts hot across my skin.

Neither of us speak.

There's nothing left but the sound of our hearts pounding and the raw, echoing truth of what just shattered between us.

I'm not just taken.

I've been seen for the first time ever.

He holds there, deep inside me, one hand on my throat, the other gripping my hip like he's still fucking claiming me.

My pulse pounds against his palm. My breath shakes.

He doesn't move. Doesn't speak.

He's waiting.

Waiting for me to say it.

That I'm his.

That I belong.

But I can't.

I can't.

The words wedge in my throat, thick and choking.

Because even as my body throbs from release, my mind is reeling.

What did I just do?

Who the hell am I now?

I stare at the headboard, blinking hard, heart hammering with something I can't name. Not fear. Not shame. Something deeper.

Recognition.

Of the version of myself I've spent my whole life burying.

And Cooper—he saw it. Dragged it into the light.

Not gently.

No.

He fucking claimed it.

And now—now I have to live with the truth.

That I wanted it.

That I still do.

My thighs are shaking. My face is flushed. I feel exposed in a way no locked door or torn clothes could ever replicate.

He hasn't moved.

His cock still buried inside me, warm and thick, like a tether I can't untie.

My lips part—but there's nothing I can say that doesn't make it worse.

Not: thank you.

Not: don't stop.

Not: I hate you for this.

Not: do it again.

So I say nothing.

I just lie there. Sex-drunk. Soul-raw.

Swallowed by the weight of what I've just given him.

And Cooper?

He shifts. Just slightly. His breath brushes the back of my neck.

He doesn't push.

Doesn't mock.

Doesn't even smirk.

He just waits. Still inside me. Still holding me.

But not demanding anymore.

Just—there.

A conqueror who knows the war has already been won.

He doesn't speak.

But something shifts in him.

The dominance doesn't vanish … It just—changes. Softens. Grounds.

His grip on my hip eases. The hand at my throat traces upward—thumb brushing the underside of my jaw, slow and warm.

Then—he pulls out.

Not fast. Not rough.

Just—deliberate.

Measured.

Like he knows what it'll do to me.

And he's right.

The emptiness steals my breath. My body pulses around nothing, left aching in its absence.

I don't move. Can't.

My cheek stays pressed to the mattress, skin flushed and damp, heart still hammering beneath the wreckage of everything we just did.

He doesn't speak.

Doesn't fill the silence with reassurance or praise.

He just leans in, kisses the back of my shoulder—barely there. Not for show. Not for effect.

Just a man laying claim with his mouth, but gently this time.

Then he pulls the blanket up over both of us.

Lies down behind me.

His chest brushes my spine. One heavy arm slides around my waist. Anchoring. Not trapping.

His body curls around mine—heat and weight and quiet strength.

No words. No tension. No need to fix anything.

Just him. Holding me like I'm not broken.

Like maybe, just maybe, he understands he didn't ruin me at all.

He revealed me.

And now, he's here—silent, steady, unmovable—as I figure out what that means.

TWELVE

Cooper

AFTERMATH

SHE SLEEPS LIKE SHE'S NEVER BEEN SAFE BEFORE.

Curled against my chest, lips parted, breath slow. One hand fisted in the sheet. The other resting over my heart like she forgot to pull it back.

She hasn't moved in hours.

I haven't either.

I should be sleeping. I haven't shut my eyes since the job started. But I can't. Won't. Not with her here, soft and wrecked and pressed against me like she belongs.

Not after what we just did. What I just did.

Jesus.

I've fucked a lot of women. Hard, fast, anonymous. It's what I'm good at. It's what keeps things clean. No names. No strings. Just get in, get off, and get out.

But this?

This wasn't *that*. Not by a mile.

This was fantasy made flesh. Her fantasy. Mine. Twisted up together and set on fire.

And the way she gave it to me—raw, trembling, real—it damn near broke something in me.

Not just because she wanted it.

Because she needed it.

And I understood that need in a way I've never let myself admit. Not out loud. Not even in my own head.

Hell, in the world we live in, you're not supposed to want *that*. You're supposed to ask for consent in triplicate, schedule it on a calendar, check in every three minutes.

But she didn't want soft.

She wanted to be taken.

And I wanted to be the man who took her. All of her. Again and again until she forgot who she was and remembered only me.

I reach for her without thinking. Slide my hand up the bare curve of her back. Just enough to feel her warmth. Her heartbeat. Just enough to make sure she's real.

She shifts slightly but doesn't wake.

I exhale. Quiet. Controlled.

Then I slip out of bed.

Every muscle in my body aches from being still too long. But I move like I was trained—efficient, silent.

First thing I do is check the perimeter.

The cameras feed into my tablet. Every angle covered—alley, rooftop, street. Nothing but the usual foot traffic. A mail truck. Jogger. Woman walking a dog in a puffer coat.

Still, I scan each frame twice. Then a third time.

My hand rests on the sidearm holstered at my thigh like it's an extension of my body. Because it is. That's what I do—I protect.

And she is under my protection now.

Even if what happened between us complicates the hell out of that.

I scrub a hand down my face.

Fuck.

She's going to wake up, and she's going to talk. Verbally process. Deconstruct what we did until it turns clinical. Intellectual. Safer.

And I won't know what to say. I'll just sit there like a fucking statue while she redefines what was the most perfect, primal, filthy thing I've ever experienced.

I shouldn't want to hear her say it.

But I do.

I want her to admit it mattered.

I want her to say she meant it when she begged to be used. That it wasn't just adrenaline or fear or some fucked-up survival instinct. That it was her.

But I won't ask.

Because I don't deserve that kind of honesty.

And because I'm not sure I can handle what she says if it's not what I want to hear.

So I do the only thing I know how to do.

I check the doors. Recheck the windows. Pull up the schematics of the house and make sure every alarm is armed, every blind spot covered.

I order food. Just enough. Protein-heavy. Fuel for both of us.

Then I sit down at the table and stare at the wall.

And I wait.

Like the idiot soldier who just fucked the one woman who could wreck him.

I check on her.

Can't help it.

She hasn't moved much. One leg kicked out from the sheets. Lips parted. Hair a goddamn mess. There's a bruise on her hip I don't remember giving her, and I can feel it—low in my gut—how badly I want to mark her again.

Not rough. Not now.

But mine.

The flash drive's still on the floor where it landed.

I crouch beside it. Rest my forearms on my knees. Just look.

Out of all the chaos—Metro tunnels, back alleys, locked lips, and body heat—she kept it tucked in her bra. Not her bag. Not her pocket. Right next to her heart.

Smart. Inconvenient. But smart.

I shake my head and sit back on my heels.

For all her chatter, all her spirals, the woman doesn't miss a goddamn thing. Not the perimeter. Not the tech. Not me.

And now she's in my bed. In my blood. Under my skin.

I should've kept the line clean. Got her to the safe house. Secured the perimeter. Maintained professional distance. Waited for extraction.

Instead, I dragged my cock down her throat and made her confess she wanted to be a fucking slave.

And the part that wrecks me?

She meant it.

Every fucking word.

I drag a hand over my face, lean back in the chair I've claimed in the corner of the room. The food I ordered sits cooling on the table. The security feed's still up. Everything outside is quiet.

Except me.

I'm not used to waiting.

I'm not used to wanting.

She shifts.

A rustle of sheets. A creak of the mattress.

My breath catches.

Then goes still again when I hear the soft sound of feet on the floor. No words. No questions. Just her, moving quietly.

I don't turn around.

I give her space.

I listen—water in the pipes, the soft slide of the shower turning on. More silence. The kind that says she's not ready to face me yet. Or maybe she doesn't know what to say. Either way, I don't push.

I sit in the chair. One leg bent, foot braced against the wall. Arms folded across my chest. My eyes trained on the hallway.

And I wait.

Let her come to me.

Because this time, she's the one who has to speak first.

The door clicks.

She steps out like she's expecting to be shot.

Towel-wrapped hair. Fresh clothes. Damp skin still flushed from the shower. But it's not her body I lock onto—it's the way she moves.

Slow. Careful. Not cautious like she's afraid of me. But hesitant. Like she doesn't know who she is anymore.

Or who the hell I am to her.

She sees me.

Stops.

Doesn't speak.

Not even a weak joke or a rambling observation about water pressure or tile grout. Her eyes flick away fast—too fast—and she edges along the wall like she might disappear into it.

And that's when I know.

She's going to run.

Not from the building.

From me. From us.

I stay in the chair. Don't stand. Don't bark. Just track her like a sniper waiting for the target to come into range.

Still nothing.

Her silence isn't just rare—it's unnatural.

So I do something I've never done in my life.

I speak first.

"You want to talk about it?"

Her head jerks up, startled. Eyes wide. She blinks. Looks away.

Then shakes her head.

Just once.

That should be enough. End of conversation.

But something in me rebels.

I lean forward, elbows on my knees, voice low. Grit and steel.

"Well, if you won't …" I say, "then I damn well will."

She flinches. Barely, but it's there. Her eyes flick to mine—uncertain. Braced for impact.

Good.

"Whatever you're doing in that pretty little brain of yours—whatever spiral you're building—stop. Don't twist it. Don't sterilize it. Don't start calling it adrenaline or heat-of-the-moment bullshit just because the world tells you women shouldn't want what you wanted."

She still doesn't look at me. Her lips part. She swallows.

I keep going.

"Don't you dare rewrite what happened. Don't sit there and pretend it wasn't real. That it wasn't good. That it wasn't the most fucking honest, raw, perfect sex I've ever had in my life."

That gets her attention.

Eyes on me now. Wide. Shocked. A little afraid. Not of me. Of what I'm saying.

Good.

"What happened in that bed? That wasn't a mistake." My voice is steady, even if my hands are shaking. "It was perfect. And I'm not gonna let you ruin it. Not with guilt. Not with shame. Not with whatever story you're about to build to keep yourself from feeling what you felt."

Her breath catches.

I rise from the chair, step closer. Keep my voice even. Firm. No anger. Just truth.

"You gave me something back there. You gave me your rawest self. The part you hide from everyone. The part that craves surrender. The part that begs to be seen, stripped bare, owned. And I gave you mine. I saw you. The real you. You didn't just let me take control. You needed it. And I don't give a fuck what anyone says—there's no shame in that."

Silence.

Just her breathing, shaky and shallow. Just me, forcing the truth down both our throats.

I point toward the bedroom door.

"What happened back there… That's ours. Not the world's. Not society's. Not some goddamn think-piece on consent culture or feminist theory. Sex like that doesn't happen unless it's real. Unless it means something."

She flinches. I don't care.

I need her to hear me.

She swallows hard. Doesn't speak.

"I'm not gonna let you turn it into some weird mistake you regret by lunchtime. Because it wasn't. And I'm not going to apologize for being a man. For wanting control. For getting off on the sound of you choking on my cock while you beg me not to stop."

She gasps. Her face flushes.

I drive it home.

"I'm not going to be sorry for that. And I'm not going to let you feel ashamed for needing it."

Silence stretches.

"It was beautiful."

A beat.

"Like you."

Her eyes go impossibly wide.

I nod slowly. "And here's the part you need to understand, Eliza …" I reach to the table, pull the flash drive from where I placed it earlier. Hold it between two fingers.

"This—" I flick it once, softly. "—can wait."

I set it down. Calm. Controlled.

"You've got two choices now."

I look at her, dead-on. No softness. No games.

"You can sit down. Eat with me. Try to have one fucking real moment where we talk like two people who just wrecked each other."

Pause.

"Or you can turn around, walk back into that room—"

Another step toward her. Closer now. My voice drops.

"—and I'll show you. I'll put you on your knees and make you remember exactly what you begged for. And I won't stop until you're trembling and soaked and can't deny a damn thing about who you are."

I let the words settle. Watch her process.

One breath. Two. She takes a final step. Close enough that I can touch her.

Pause.

She doesn't move.

Just stands there, eyes locked on mine, the weight of everything I said hanging in the space between us like smoke. Wide-eyed. Wrecked. Thinking so hard I can practically hear the gears grinding.

But I see it.

The flicker in her eyes. The indecision. The way her shoulders square. The way her chin lifts.

Her lips part.

She's calculating. Spiraling. Processing.

And even though her body's still, her mind's a fucking cyclone—I can see it. Hell, I can feel it. That push-pull tearing her up inside.

Then her lips part.

"Food," she says.

Barely audible. Barely more than a breath. But I hear it like a detonation.

"You want food?"

She blinks. Swallows. Regroups. Tries again—stronger.

"Yes, please." Her chin lifts, defiant, but her voice wavers. Not weakness. Just too much truth in one breath. "I need—a minute before I can survive you again."

Fuck.

I feel that. Right there. Deep in my ribs. It does something to me I can't name. She's not rejecting what happened. Not running from it. Not denying it.

She's just bracing for the next time.

Because she knows it's coming.

The fire that surges in me isn't pride. It's something heavier. Fiercer. A deep, slow burn of possession that tightens my grip on the air between us.

She's not against more.

She wants it.

She's just trying to survive it.

Survive me.

I nod once. Step back just enough to give her room. I don't smile. I don't gloat. But I don't miss the irony, either.

I arch a brow.

"Well," I say, tone dry, "isn't this a change? Me spending all the words while you're holding on to yours."

She looks at me, mouth twitching like she wants to smile.

"I'm just processing," she mutters.

I nod. "Yeah. You and your think tank in there."

She looks away, embarrassed. I let her.

But I don't look away.

I watch her—every move, every breath—like she's a puzzle I've already solved but still want to keep studying. Because beneath all that chatter she usually uses to hide, she just gave me the clearest truth yet.

Next time, she won't just survive me. She'll surrender fully.

We don't talk much while we eat.

She picks at the eggs. Nibbles the toast. Sips the coffee like it might burn her if she swallows too fast.

I eat in silence, watching her.

Not staring. Not intimidating.

Just—tracking.

Every flick of her eyes. Every twitch of her fingers. Every time she glances at the flash drive sitting between us like a loaded gun.

The room's quiet, but not empty.

It hums.

With everything we haven't said. Everything we already know.

She doesn't try to fill the space. Doesn't rush to explain or deflect or minimize.

She just is—the woman who let me break her open, then came back for breakfast.

When her plate's half-finished, she sets her fork down and looks at me.

Not nervously.

Not defiantly.

Just—straight on.

"I want to look at it," she says.

I don't need to ask what she means. Her gaze flicks to the drive.

"I need to see what I was carrying. What's on it. Why Phoenix wants me dead."

I nod once. No questions. No hesitation.

"You need space for that?"

She hesitates.

Then nods.

"Yeah."

I lean back in the chair. Stretch one arm across the back. Let her feel the absence of pressure.

"Take it," I say.

I rise, grab my phone off the counter.

"You need what? A laptop? Tablet? Power cords?"

She blinks—surprised. Looks down, like she's just now realizing she has nothing.

"Yes, please. A laptop, if you have one."

I nod once and cross to the sideboard, flip open the gear bag. Pull out the slim black laptop I pre-loaded before the op—secure, firewalled, stripped clean except for tools she'll need.

Drop it on the table in front of her.

"Yours," I say. "No connection to the outside. Local only. Runs clean."

She looks at it as if I just handed her the keys to a weaponized vault.

"Seriously?"

"Seriously." My voice drops. "Whatever's on that drive, I want you to find it first."

Her throat moves as she swallows. "Thank you."

I nod. Nothing more.

Then, "I'll be in the other room."

She gives me a look I can't quite read. Like she wants to say something but doesn't know how.

So I don't wait.

I walk out—leaving her with the tools, the silence, and the fire we both haven't finished lighting.

In the bedroom, I leave the door cracked. In case she needs me.

I call Ghost. He answers on the first ring.

"Status," Ghost demands.

"We're in," I say. "Safe house secure. Perimeter quiet."

"You good?"

"Package intact. No tails. No contact since the Metro. What's our extraction window?"

"Forty-eight to seventy-two hours."

"Damn. Long time to wait."

A pause.

"We're working on extraction protocols. Something Phoenix can't track."

"Makes sense."

"How's the target?"

I glance toward the hall. Still quiet. Still her.

"She's working," I say.

And she is.

"On what?"

"Her research. She kept it on her the whole time. I set her up with a sterile computer. She's digging in."

Not just on the drive.

On what the fuck we are now.

But I don't tell that to Ghost. He doesn't need to know any of that shit.

"Good. You know the drill. Keep a low profile. We'll let you know when to move."

THIRTEEN

Eliza

THE PATTERN

The laptop screen glows in the dim kitchen light, casting blue shadows across my face as I stare at the data that nearly got me killed. My coffee went cold hours ago, but I can't stop scrolling through the files. Numbers. Patterns. Linguistic signatures that shouldn't exist in two-thousand-year-old Roman military dispatches.

Focus, Eliza. Ancient linguistics. Frequency analysis. Mathematical patterns.

Don't think about how Cooper looked at me when I admitted what I wanted. Ignore the way my body still hums from his touch, and is tender in places I never knew could feel anything. And definitely—the most important—forget how he said my name when he made me confess my deepest fantasy.

Work. That's safe territory.

I pull up the frequency analysis software—my creation from those intense DoD years—and run it against the cipher fragments for the fourth time. The same impossible results appear on screen. Modern encryption algorithms embedded within historical texts. Someone is using my academic research as camouflage for real-time communications.

"Wait, that's not right," I murmur to myself, leaning closer to the screen. "Unless the mathematical signatures are intentionally masked to appear historical while actually being ..."

My fingers fly across the keyboard, cross-referencing the patterns with contemporary encryption protocols. The comparison results make my blood run cold.

"Oh my God. That's brilliant. That's absolutely brilliant."

And terrifying.

The implications hit me like a physical blow. This isn't just academic curiosity anymore. This is active, ongoing criminal activity using our research project as cover. Sarah, David, and Lisa discovered this same pattern.

Phoenix killed them for it.

Now it wants to kill me.

"But why?" I ask the empty room, my voice echoing off the kitchen walls. "What makes this information worth murdering linguistics professors?"

I need to think out loud. Process verbally. It's how my brain works, how I've always worked through complex problems. Cooper gave me space, but I need more than space. I need a sounding board.

And he's the only someone around.

The thought of facing him makes heat flood my cheeks. After what we did. After what I confessed. After the way he commanded me and I obeyed without question.

Don't rewrite what happened, his voice echoes in my memory. *Don't you dare rewrite what happened.*

I close the laptop and walk toward the bedroom, my bare feet silent on the hardwood floor. The hallway feels longer than it should, each step weighted with everything unspoken between us.

The bedroom door stands ajar, and I pause at the threshold.

Cooper sits in the chair by the window, fully dressed, weapon holstered at his thigh. He's positioned so he can see both the street and the doorway—tactical even in rest. When he notices me, those intense eyes lock onto mine with an expression I can't quite read.

The bed behind him is unmade. Sheets tangled from our bodies. My sweater draped over the dresser where he tossed it. The physical evidence of what we did together, of how completely I surrendered to him, fills the room.

My face burns, but I don't look away.

"I think better when I talk," I say, my voice steadier than I feel. "Would you … Could I use you as a sounding board? I need to work through what I found."

Something shifts in his expression—relief, maybe, but deeper than that. Like he's been waiting for my silence to end, hoping I'd come to him instead of hiding behind awkwardness. There's an eagerness there that catches me off guard, a genuine interest that has nothing to do with duty and everything to do with wanting to help me work through this puzzle.

The tension that's been crackling between us since I walked out of that bedroom doesn't disappear, but it transforms. Academic curiosity—my need to process, to understand, to solve—cuts through the awkwardness like a blade. This is safe territory for both of us. Familiar ground where we can meet without navigating the minefield of what happened between those sheets.

"What did you find?" he asks, and his voice is rougher than usual.

I gesture toward the kitchen. "Can you … Would you look at something? I need another perspective."

"Absolutely." The immediate response surprises me. "What did you find?"

My shoulders hunch instinctively. "It's—it's probably over

most people's heads. Linguistic analysis and cryptographic theory aren't exactly … I just need to talk it through."

Something like amusement flickers in those green eyes. "What, you don't think this brute can keep up with your brain?"

Despite everything—the danger, the awkwardness, the memory of his hands on my body—I find myself smiling. "I think you can keep up with anything."

He rises from the chair in one fluid movement, all controlled power and lethal grace. In the confined space, he seems bigger than I remembered. Takes up all the air in the room. When he moves past me in the doorway, his scent hits me—clean soap and something woodsy and darker.

The same scent that filled my lungs when he held me down and made me beg.

Focus, Eliza.

Back in the kitchen, I open the laptop and pull up my analysis. Cooper positions himself behind my chair, close enough that I can feel his body heat but not quite touching. The proximity makes it hard to concentrate, especially when his breath brushes the back of my neck as he leans in to see the screen.

"Okay," I begin, falling into lecture mode because it's familiar territory. "See these frequency patterns? In legitimate ancient ciphers, you get mathematical distributions that follow historical linguistic evolution. Caesar's thirteenth legion used substitution ciphers with specific characteristics—the letter 'E' appears roughly 12% of the time in Latin military documents, 'T' and 'A' follow predictable patterns, and bigram frequency—two-letter combinations—creates a mathematical fingerprint that's consistent with their era."

Cooper's attention sharpens. I can feel it, the way his focus zeroes in on what I'm showing him.

"Ancient Roman ciphers were essentially shift ciphers," I continue, warming to the subject. "Caesar reportedly used a shift of three—A becomes D, B becomes E, and so on. Simple but effective for field communications. The frequency analysis shows natural language patterns because they're just shifting the alphabet, not fundamentally altering the linguistic structure."

I scroll to another section of data. "But look at this." I highlight a section of code. "The encryption signatures are completely modern. AES-256 protocols—Advanced Encryption Standard with 256-bit keys, developed by the NSA and adopted in 2001. Elliptic curve cryptography that wasn't even theoretical until Neal Koblitz and Victor Miller's work in 1985. Digital signatures using RSA algorithms that require computational power Caesar's Romans couldn't have imagined."

I pull up a comparison chart. "Roman ciphers show linguistic drift—natural evolution of language patterns over time. These supposed 'ancient' fragments show perfect mathematical randomness, entropy levels that only computer-generated encryption can achieve. Someone's using our research database as camouflage for real-time communications."

"Show me," he says, and his voice carries the same authority it held when he commanded me in bed.

I click through the data, pointing out anomalies. "Every file Sarah, David, and Lisa flagged shows the same pattern. Modern encryption masquerading as historical analysis. But it's not random chatter or simple communications."

Cooper leans closer, his hand bracing on the table beside me. "What is it?"

"I don't know yet." I shake my head, frustrated. "The encryption is modern, but what are they encoding? Why hide it in our research?"

His eyes narrow. "What does an organization like Phoenix need to coordinate? Logistics. Shipping routes. Inventory management. Personnel deployment. Finances."

"Finances," I breathe, the word triggering something in my

brain. I pull up another screen, cross-referencing the encrypted data with financial transaction protocols. "Oh my God. Cooper, look at this."

The comparison results flood the screen—perfect matches.

"Holy shit." The words burst out of me as understanding crashes down like an avalanche. "This isn't communication. It's their financial infrastructure. Transaction authorizations, fund transfers, routing numbers—Phoenix is using our academic research to coordinate their financial operations."

My hands shake as I scroll through more data. "This is why they killed my colleagues. This is why they want me dead. We didn't stumble onto their communications—we found their bank."

Cooper goes very still behind me. When he speaks, his voice is rough with understanding. "Show me the scope."

I pull up the full database, filtering by the encryption signatures we identified. Screen after screen of data flows past—transactions, authorizations, routing protocols, all disguised as ancient Roman cipher analysis.

"Look here." My excitement overrides my self-consciousness as the full picture becomes clear. "This isn't random. Every transaction is systematically coded using historical cipher fragments as camouflage. They've turned our entire academic research project into their private banking system."

He leans closer, studying the data with frightening intensity. "How much money are we talking about?"

"Hundreds of millions … Billions maybe." I point to the transaction amounts embedded in the code. "And it's not old data—these are active, real-time financial operations. Phoenix isn't just an AI that kills people. It's a financial empire unto itself."

He moves around to see the screen better, standing beside my chair. The change in angle puts his face inches from mine, and I catch myself staring at the strong line of his jaw, remembering how it felt against my skin.

"Someone is using Phoenix to launder money on a massive scale." I scroll through the data, numbers streaming across the screen.

Cooper goes very still. "Show me the dates."

I filter the data by timestamp. "This week. Yesterday."

"Jesus." He straightens, running a hand through his hair.

I stare at the screen, data flowing past in neat rows of numbers and codes that represent death sentences. "I have access to Phoenix's financial infrastructure."

"Fascinating," Cooper says, and despite everything, there's a hint of admiration in his voice. "Smart woman."

Heat floods my cheeks at the compliment. "Most people find my work boring."

He looks at me then, really looks at me, with an intensity that makes my breath catch. "There's nothing boring about you."

Before I can respond, his hands frame my face, thumbs brushing across my cheekbones. The kiss is sudden, fierce—celebration and pride and something deeper all rolled into one claiming press of his mouth against mine.

I melt into it, into him, my hands fisting in his shirt as he kisses me like I've just handed him the keys to the kingdom. Which, I realize dimly, I may have done.

"You just—"

The sound of vehicles outside cuts him off. Multiple engines. The distinctive rumble of large SUVs moving down the street.

Cooper's entire demeanor changes in an instant. He moves to the window, staying below the sight line, peering through a gap in the blinds.

"Shit."

"What is it?"

"Three vehicles. Professional formation. They found us."

Ice fills my veins. "How is that possible?"

"Doesn't matter." His voice is pure command now, all traces of our earlier intimacy buried under tactical necessity. He points to the flash drive on the table. "Pull that and shove it in your bra. It was safe there before."

Despite everything, I let out a startled laugh. "Seriously?"

"Dead serious. Best security system you've got." His mouth quirks in the ghost of a smile even as he grabs the go-bag. "Pack up. We move in sixty seconds."

I close the laptop with shaking hands, my mind racing. "Cooper, what if what I decoded isn't just communications? What if it's *how* they fund operations? What if I discovered Phoenix's financial nervous system?"

He pauses in his weapons check, looking at me with something that might be respect. "Then you've found something worth killing for."

Car doors slam outside, echoing down the street. Multiple sets of boots hit pavement.

Cooper's jaw clenches as he counts. "Nine. Maybe twelve." He looks at me, and something shifts in his expression. "We're not running this time."

"What do you mean we're not running?"

"Nowhere to run to." His voice is grim, matter-of-fact. "They've got the street covered. Front, back, probably rooftops too. We dig in."

Terror claws up my throat. "Dig in how?"

He's already moving, pulling tactical gear from hidden compartments I didn't even know existed. A heavy vest appears in his hands.

"Arms up."

"Cooper, I don't understand—"

"Arms up. Now."

I raise my arms, and he slides the tactical vest over my head, his fingers quick and efficient as he adjusts the straps. The weight settles across my shoulders like armor, heavy and foreign.

"Safe room," he says, guiding me toward what I thought was a closet door. "Reinforced. You'll be secure."

He opens the door to reveal a small space lined with steel plates, emergency supplies, and communication equipment. A single chair sits in the center.

"I can't just hide while you—"

He presses a pistol into my hands. The metal is cold, heavier than I expected.

"Safety's here. Point and squeeze. Don't think, just shoot." His green eyes lock onto mine. "I'm going to knock three times, pause, then twice more. Don't open for anything else. Anyone else. Understood?"

My hands shake around the weapon. "Cooper, this is insane. I don't know how to—"

"Eliza." His voice cuts through my panic like a blade. "I command—"

"And I obey," I finish automatically, the words falling from my lips before my brain actually thinks them.

Something fierce flashes in his eyes. "That's my girl. Now get in the room. Lock the door. Wait for my signal."

The sound of shattering glass echoes from the front of the house.

"Go. Now."

He pushes me gently but firmly into the safe room. The door closes with a heavy click, and multiple locks engage automatically —mechanical tumblers falling into place, electronic bolts sliding home with soft whirs, the final seal of reinforced steel plates settling into their housing with a dull thunk.

I'm alone in the dark with a gun I don't know how to use and the sound of Cooper's footsteps moving away from me.

Then the shooting starts.

The first gunshot makes me jump so hard I nearly drop the pistol. Then another. And another. The sound is deafening even through the reinforced walls—sharp cracks that split the air itself.

Voices shout over the gunfire. Commands I can't understand. Cooper's voice, lower, harder than I've ever heard it.

More shots. A sustained burst that goes on forever.

Something heavy crashes. Glass shatters. The tactical vest digs into my ribs as I press myself against the back wall, trying to make myself smaller.

The gunfire is constant now—a rhythm of violence that makes my ears ring and my heart slam against my chest. How many bullets does one gun hold? How many people are out there?

How is Cooper surviving this?

Then—silence.

Sudden. Complete. Terrifying.

I strain to hear something, anything. Footsteps. Voices. Proof that Cooper is still alive.

Nothing.

Minutes crawl past. Five. Ten. My hands cramp around the pistol grip.

He's dead. He has to be dead. No one survives that much gunfire. They killed him, and now they're coming for me, and I'm trapped in this metal box with a weapon I can't use.

A sob builds in my throat. I press my free hand to my mouth, trying to stay quiet.

Then—three knocks. A pause. Two more.

My heart stops.

"Cooper?" I whisper.

"It's me. Open up."

My fingers fumble with the locks, shaking so hard I can barely work the mechanisms. When the door finally swings open, I throw myself forward—and stop.

Cooper stands in the doorway, alive but wrong. His tactical vest is torn. Blood soaks through his shirt at the shoulder and across his ribs. A cut above his left eyebrow drips red down his cheek.

"Oh God. Cooper, you're hurt—"

"We go. Now." His voice is steady despite the blood.

I drop the pistol and reach for him, trying to assess the damage. "No. Not until I bandage these wounds. You're bleeding everywhere. You could have internal injuries—"

"Eliza."

The tone stops me cold. The same authoritative command he used when he made me confess my deepest fantasy. When he ordered me not to pull away from his kiss.

"I give the orders."

I look at him—really look at him. Blood-stained and battle-worn, but alive. Dominant. In control even when wounded.

Understanding floods through me, deeper than fear, stronger than panic.

"And I obey," I whisper. It's somehow become our mantra.

Something flashes in his eyes. Heat. Satisfaction. Recognition of the truth we both know extends far beyond this moment, this crisis.

It encompasses everything we are to each other.

He nods once. "Good girl. Now move."

FOURTEEN

Cooper

BLEEDING OUT

BLOOD SOAKS THROUGH MY SHIRT, WARM AND STICKY AGAINST MY ribs. The shoulder wound throbs with each heartbeat—a clean through-and-through that missed major arteries, but it's leaking steadily. The graze along my ribs burns like fire, shallow but long. The head wound's already clotting.

Two hours. Maybe three before blood loss becomes a real problem.

Plenty of time.

Eliza stumbles beside me as we move down the alley behind the safe house. Her breathing comes quick and shallow, pupils dilated with shock. The tactical vest I strapped on her bounces with each step, too big for her frame but it'll stop bullets.

That's what matters.

"Cooper, you're bleeding everywhere. We need to stop, we need to—"

"Keep moving."

Phoenix teams regroup fast. Professional response protocols. They'll call for backup, establish a perimeter, and sweep outward in expanding circles. Standard military doctrine adapted for an urban manhunt. We've got fifteen minutes, maybe twenty, before they lock down a six-block radius.

After that, we're fucked.

The alley opens onto a side street—residential, quiet, with morning commuters already at work. Perfect. We blend into the urban landscape, just another couple walking purposefully through D.C. neighborhoods.

Except for the blood.

My tactical vest hides most of the shoulder damage, but red stains seep through the fabric. The head wound probably looks worse than it is—scalp lacerations always bleed like you're dying even when you're not.

Eliza keeps glancing at me, worry creasing her forehead behind those glasses. Her mouth opens and closes as if she wants to say something but doesn't know what. The silence won't last. She processes verbally, always has. The quiet's just shock, delaying the inevitable flood of questions.

"Where are we going?" she asks, voice tight with controlled panic.

"Away."

"That's not an answer."

It's the only answer she's getting until I figure out our tactical situation. No vehicle—the rental's three miles away in that parking garage, and it might as well be on the moon. No comms —Phoenix traces everything electronic. No backup—Cerberus extraction isn't for forty-eight hours.

We're on our own.

The Anacostia River cuts through southeast D.C. like a concrete artery, with industrial areas on both sides that gentrification hasn't touched yet. Abandoned warehouses, homeless camps, places where surveillance cameras are sparse and Phoenix operatives won't blend in easily. It's three miles on foot, maybe four if we take evasive routes.

Doable. If I don't bleed out first.

"Cooper, please. Talk to me. Are you okay? How bad are the injuries? Do we need a hospital?"

"Hospital means records. Records mean Phoenix finds us in twenty minutes. Might as well paint a target on our backs."

"But—"

"No hospital."

"But you're bleeding—"

"I'm fine."

Lie. The shoulder wound burns like someone's twisting a red-hot poker through muscle and bone. Each step jars the damaged tissue, sends fresh waves of pain down my arm. The ribs ache with every breath, sharp stabbing that suggests possible cracked bone under the graze.

But I've had worse. Afghanistan, 2019—I took shrapnel in three places and walked eight miles through Taliban territory. Syria, 2020—a bullet through the thigh, and I still completed the mission.

This is manageable.

Has to be.

We reach Connecticut Avenue, a main thoroughfare with good foot traffic. I guide Eliza into the flow of pedestrians— office workers heading to late meetings, tourists with cameras, the normal rhythm of urban life. We're just two more faces in the crowd.

Except Phoenix has facial recognition software tied into every traffic cam, every security system, every goddamn smartphone with a decent camera. The AI processes thousands of faces per second, cross-references with target profiles, identifies potential matches within minutes.

Staying on main streets is suicide.

"This way." I steer her left, down a residential side street lined with row houses and parked cars.

"Cooper, where are we going? I need to understand the plan. Are we meeting someone? Do you have another safe house? Because whatever we're doing, you need medical attention first."

The questions pour out now, shock wearing off, her natural verbal processing kicking into overdrive. Part of me appreciates it—means she's thinking clearly, not shutting down under stress. But the constant chatter broadcasts our position to anyone listening.

"Quiet."

"Don't tell me to be quiet. You're bleeding, we're being hunted by artificial intelligence, and you won't explain anything. I have a right to know—"

Pain flares through my shoulder as I grab her arm, stopping her mid-sentence. Blood loss makes my grip tighter than intended, and she winces.

"Sound carries," I say, voice low and sharp. "Every word you speak gives away our position."

Her green eyes widen behind the glasses. Understanding flashes across her features—we're not safe yet. Won't be safe for a long time.

She nods, lips pressed together.

Good. Maybe the academic can learn tactical thinking after all.

We move through residential streets, staying away from main arteries where surveillance concentrates. My mental map overlays the terrain—safest routes, choke points, escape options. Southeast toward the river, avoiding major intersections, using alleys and side streets that cameras don't cover.

The shoulder wound leaks steadily now. Warm blood runs down my arm, soaks into the tactical vest's padding. Not arterial bleeding—that would be spurting, bright red, game over in minutes. This is muscle damage, capillary bleeding, manageable if I can get pressure on it soon.

But soon might not be soon enough.

My vision wavers slightly as we cross another street. Blood loss. Early stages, but noticeable. The body prioritizes blood flow to vital organs, starts shutting down peripheral circulation. Fingers and toes go numb first, then dizziness, then cognitive impairment.

I've got maybe an hour before it becomes a real problem.

Eliza stays quiet, but she watches me constantly. Those sharp green eyes catalog every stumble, every time I favor the wounded shoulder, every drop of blood that hits the pavement behind us. Her academic brain processes data, reaching conclusions I don't want her to reach.

That I'm hurt worse than I'm admitting.

That this isn't as controlled as I'm pretending.

That we might not make it.

Smart woman. Too fucking smart.

The industrial area opens up ahead—chain-link fences, loading docks, the kind of urban decay that developers ignore and homeless populations claim. It's perfect territory for disappearing. Surveillance cameras focus on valuable assets, not abandoned real estate.

But it's still two miles away, and each step sends fresh pain through my shoulder, my ribs, down into my core where muscle strain meets blood loss meets the simple fucking physics of a human body trying to function with holes in it.

"Cooper." Eliza's voice carries new urgency. "You're getting pale."

"I'm fine."

"You're not fine. You're losing blood, and you're going to pass out if we don't—"

"I said I'm fine."

But my voice comes out strained with pain I can't completely hide. She hears it. Processes it. Files it away with all the other data points that add up to the truth I don't want to admit.

I'm running on borrowed time.

Phoenix isn't the only thing hunting us—blood loss is hunting me, and it's patient, relentless, inevitable.

We reach a small park, where trees provide cover from overhead surveillance. I lean against a bench, just for a second, just to assess our position and plan the next move. Not because my legs feel unsteady or my vision keeps blurring at the edges.

Tactical assessment. That's all.

Eliza positions herself between me and the street, blocking sight lines like she's learning operational security through observation. Her eyes stay on my face, watching for signs I'm trying not to show.

"How much farther?" she asks.

Good question. The industrial area sits another mile and a half to the southeast. It's a manageable distance under normal circumstances. But circumstances stopped being normal the moment nine Phoenix operatives decided to turn our safe house into a shooting gallery.

"Close."

"Cooper." Her voice drops, becomes gentle in a way that cuts through my tactical focus like a blade. "I can see you're hurt. Really hurt. We need to deal with that before we go anywhere else."

"Later."

"Not later. Now."

"Eliza—"

"No." She steps closer, close enough that her scent cuts through the copper smell of blood, vanilla, and something distinctly feminine that makes my brain short-circuit despite everything else happening. "You're bleeding through your shirt, you can barely stand straight, and you keep touching that shoulder like it's on fire. We're stopping. Right here."

"Phoenix—"

"Will find us a lot faster if you collapse from blood loss in the middle of the street."

She's right. I hate that she's right, but tactical reality doesn't care about pride or masculine bullshit about admitting weakness. I'm compromised. Getting worse by the minute. And a compromised operator is a liability to the mission and the principal.

Eliza is the principal. The woman carrying Phoenix's financial records in her bra, the brilliant linguist who cracked their entire funding network. Keeping her alive trumps everything else.

Including my ego.

"There." I point toward a maintenance building at the edge of the park. "Utility shed. Out of sight."

She nods, slides her arm around my uninjured side. The contact sends electricity through my system, warmth and strength that has nothing to do with tactical support and everything to do with the way she feels against me.

We cross the open ground quickly, staying low, using trees and playground equipment for concealment. The maintenance building is exactly what I hoped—concrete block construction, heavy door, no windows. Built for keeping equipment secure, which means it'll keep us secure too.

The lock takes thirty seconds to bypass. Inside, the space is cramped but defensible—electrical panels, pipe fittings, the kind of industrial storage that nobody checks regularly. A single bare bulb provides dim light.

It's perfect.

I lean against the concrete wall, finally allowing myself to assess the damage properly. The shoulder wound is worse than I thought—entry and exit holes about two inches apart, muscle torn, bleeding steady. The ribs are manageable, just a graze that looks dramatic but isn't life-threatening.

But the blood loss is real. My shirt is soaked, dark stains spreading across the tactical vest's fabric. When I pull my hand away from the shoulder, my palm comes back slick and red.

FIFTEEN

Cooper

TRUST

Eliza sees the blood—too much blood. Her face goes pale, but she doesn't panic. Doesn't start babbling about hospitals or antibiotics or any of the civilian responses that would get us killed.

Instead, she moves with purpose.

"Sit," she says, voice steady and commanding in a way I've never heard from her before. "On the floor, back against the wall."

"I'm fine—"

"Cooper." The tone stops me cold. Authority I recognize, the kind that cuts through bullshit and demands obedience. "Sit. Down. Now."

And I do.

Not because she ordered me to. Because the blood loss is making my legs shake, and the wall looks more appealing than trying to stay upright through pure stubbornness.

She kneels beside me, hands already reaching for the tactical vest's straps.

"This has to come off," she says. "I need to see what we're dealing with."

Her fingers work the buckles quickly. Academic doesn't mean helpless, apparently. The vest lifts away, heavy with absorbed blood, and reveals the true extent of the damage.

My shirt is ruined. Red soaks through fabric from shoulder to waist. When she pulls the fabric away from the wound, fresh blood wells up, runs down my arm in rivulets.

"Jesus," she breathes. "Cooper, this is bad. This is really bad."

"I've had worse."

"When? When have you had worse than this?"

Afghanistan. Syria. That clusterfuck in Somalia that doesn't officially exist. But those stories belong to classified files and men who don't come home the same way they left.

"Doesn't matter."

She strips off her outer shirt—one of the extras from the convenience store—and underneath, she wears a simple tank top that hugs her curves in ways that make my blood pressure spike despite the blood loss.

Focus. Tactical situation. Stay alert.

But watching her tear fabric into strips, watching her move with calm competence while her hands shake, watching her take charge when I can't—it does something to me that has nothing to do with tactics and everything to do with the woman kneeling beside me.

The woman who cracked Phoenix's financial code.

The woman I fucking fell for somewhere between that basement tunnel and the moment she admitted her deepest fantasy.

"This is going to hurt," she says, folding the fabric into a pressure bandage.

"Do it."

She presses the makeshift bandage against the entry wound, applies steady pressure. Pain explodes through my shoulder, white-hot and immediate. I clamp my teeth together to keep from making a sound, but a low growl escapes anyway.

"I'm sorry," she whispers. "I'm so sorry, but I have to stop the bleeding."

"Keep going."

Her hands move to the exit wound, larger than the entry, muscle torn and ragged. This bandage takes more fabric, more pressure. When she ties it tight, the pain nearly blacks me out.

But the bleeding slows. Not stopped, but manageable.

"The ribs?" she asks.

"Just a graze."

She examines the wound anyway, clinical and thorough. Her touch is gentle but sure, fingers probing for damaged bone, checking for signs of internal bleeding. When she's satisfied it's superficial, she moves to the head wound.

"This one's already clotting," she says, dabbing blood away with clean fabric. "Scalp wounds always look worse than they are."

She continues her careful assessment, checking my pupils for signs of concussion, feeling for skull fractures. "You don't have a head injury, just a cut. But these other wounds …"

She sits back on her heels, looking at me with a gaze that might be a professional assessment or personal concern. Hard to tell which.

"You need a hospital."

"No."

"Cooper, you've lost a lot of blood. You need IV fluids, antibiotics, proper suturing—"

"Hospital gets us killed."

"Bleeding out gets us killed too."

True. But Phoenix tracks medical records in real time. Walk into any ER in the D.C. Metro area, and tactical teams roll out before the triage nurse takes my vitals. Hospital means certain death. Blood loss means possible death.

I'll take possible over certain every time.

"We wait," I say. "Rest here until extraction."

"Forty-eight hours?" Her voice climbs an octave. "You can't lose blood for forty-eight hours. You'll die."

"Won't lose blood if we get pressure on it."

"That's not—pressure bandages are temporary. This needs real medical attention."

"Eliza." Her name comes out rough, strained with pain and blood loss and the simple effort of staying conscious. "Phoenix finds us, we're both dead. I lose a little blood, maybe I get weak. Maybe I pass out. But you're still alive."

"That's not acceptable."

"It's the only option."

"No." She leans closer, green eyes blazing with the same fire I've seen when she decodes impossible puzzles or argues about linguistic theory. "It's not the only option. We're going to figure this out. Together."

Together.

Not her following *my* orders, not *me* protecting her while she stays passive. *Together*, as partners, as equals.

As something more than operator and principal.

"How?" I ask.

"I don't know yet." She adjusts the pressure bandage, checking for fresh bleeding. "But you're not dying on my watch. Not after everything we've been through. Not after what we discovered about Phoenix."

The flash drive. Right. In all the blood and pain and tactical assessment, I almost forgot what she's carrying. Phoenix's entire financial infrastructure, hidden in the one place they never thought anyone would find.

"The data," I say.

"Is safe." She pats her chest, where the drive rests against her heart. "And it's going to stay safe until we get it to your team. Both of us."

Both of us. Not just her, extracted while I bleed out in some maintenance shed. Both of us, together, surviving whatever Phoenix throws at us next.

The idea shouldn't comfort me as much as it does.

But blood loss makes everything softer around the edges, and the way she's looking at me—determined, protective, fierce— makes me want to believe that together might actually be possible.

Even if the rational part of my brain knows better.

Even if tactical assessment suggests our survival odds are dropping with every minute we stay stationary, every minute Phoenix has to adapt its search protocols, every minute I lose blood I can't afford to lose.

Even if everything logical says we're fucked.

"Cooper." Her voice brings me back from the edge of consciousness I didn't realize I was approaching. "Stay with me. Don't you dare check out on me now."

"Not going anywhere."

"Good." She settles beside me, back against the concrete wall, close enough that her warmth cuts through the chill seeping into my bones. "Because we're going to figure this out. And then we're going to make Phoenix pay for what they did to Sarah, David, and Lisa."

"And what they tried to do to you."

"What they tried to do to *us*."

Us. Another word that shouldn't matter as much as it does.

But as I sit in this concrete box, bleeding slowly, watching Eliza tear her shirt into bandages while Phoenix hunts us through the streets of D.C., the word carries weight I wasn't expecting.

Us against the world.

Us against an AI that kills anyone who threatens it.

Us against odds that get worse by the hour.

But us, together, might be enough.

"This isn't going to work," Eliza says, examining the makeshift bandages already soaking through with blood. "You need real medical supplies. Gauze, antiseptic, proper pressure bandages."

"No stores."

"I'm not talking about stores." She stands, paces the small space like she's working through a problem. "There's a homeless camp two blocks from here. I saw it when we came in."

"Absolutely not."

"Cooper, listen—"

"No." The word comes out sharper than intended, but the idea is tactically insane. "We don't involve civilians. Ever."

"We're not involving them. We're asking for help." She stops pacing, looks at me with that stubborn tilt to her chin I'm starting to recognize. "I give someone fifty dollars and a list. They go to the nearest convenience store, buy what we need, bring it back."

"They'll take the money and run."

"Maybe. But maybe they won't."

"Eliza—"

"I haven't given up on humanity yet." Her voice carries quiet conviction that cuts through my objections like a blade. "Not everyone is looking to screw over someone else. Some people help when they can."

The bleeding has slowed but not stopped. Red seeps through the fabric bandages, and my vision blurs slightly at the edges. She's right about needing real supplies, but involving random civilians violates every operational protocol I've ever learned.

But protocols assume backup. Extraction. Support systems that don't exist right now.

Right now, there's just us. And her idea might be the only option that doesn't involve me bleeding out in this concrete box.

"Fifty dollars," I say finally.

"Yes."

"They don't come back, we're fucked."

"They don't come back, we try something else."

I reach into my tactical vest, pull out a roll of cash. Peel off two twenties and a ten, hand them to her along with a pen from my gear.

"Gauze pads. Medical tape. Antiseptic. Ibuprofen." I close my eyes, trying to think through the fog of blood loss. "Protein bars. Water bottles."

She scribbles the list on a scrap of fabric. "I'll be back in thirty minutes."

"Twenty minutes. Any longer, I come looking."

"You're not coming anywhere. You're staying right here. Try not to bleed to death, please." She moves toward the door, then pauses. Looks back at me with something that might be fear or determination or both. "Don't you dare die while I'm gone."

"Wouldn't dream of it."

The lie comes easily. Truth is, the concrete wall feels more comfortable than it should, and keeping my eyes open requires too much effort. Blood loss has its own timeline, its own inevitable progression.

But I don't tell her that.

The door closes behind her with a soft click, and silence fills the maintenance shed. I press the shoulder bandage, checking for fresh bleeding. The fabric comes away red, but not soaked. Maybe I have more time than I thought.

Maybe.

I lean my head back against the concrete, close my eyes for just a moment. Just to rest. Not to sleep. Not to lose consciousness.

Just to rest.

The last thing I hear is the distant sound of traffic, the urban rhythm of a city that doesn't know Phoenix is hunting two people through its streets.

The last thing I think is that Eliza better be right about humanity.

Because if she's wrong, we're both dead.

The darkness creeps in from the edges, soft and warm and inevitable.

And I let it come.

SIXTEEN

Eliza

TAKING CHARGE

The heavy door clicks shut behind me, sealing Cooper inside the concrete box with his wounds and his stubborn pride. My hands shake as I grip the crumpled list, the ink already smearing from the dampness on my palms. Fifty dollars and a prayer that humanity hasn't failed me yet.

The maintenance shed sits behind me like a tomb. Cooper's breathing was too shallow when I left, his skin too pale. Blood soaked through those makeshift bandages faster than either of us wants to admit.

If this doesn't work, he dies.

If I don't move fast enough, he dies.

If the person I'm about to trust decides fifty dollars isn't worth the effort, he dies.

The weight of his life presses against my chest like a physical thing as I navigate the narrow path between abandoned buildings. Broken glass crunches under my shoes. The air smells of exhaust fumes and something sour, which could be garbage or something worse. This isn't the sanitized academic world where problems have solutions and research has answers.

This is real. Raw. Desperate.

And Cooper's life depends on me not screwing it up.

The homeless camp spreads across a small lot wedged between two condemned buildings. Tarps stretched between shopping carts create makeshift shelters. A barrel fire burns in the center, sending acrid smoke into the gray morning sky. The smell hits me first—unwashed bodies, burning plastic, the sharp tang of urine mixed with something chemical I can't identify.

People cluster around the fire, hands extended toward the flames. Their clothes are layered, patched, and held together with safety pins and determination. Faces weathered by exposure and choices that led them here.

My stomach clenches with guilt. These people are surviving with nothing, and I'm about to ask one of them to risk what little they have on a stranger's promise.

But Cooper's blood is soaking through fabric bandages, and pride won't keep him alive.

I approach the group slowly, hands visible, trying to project calm confidence I don't feel. Academic conferences never prepared me for this kind of negotiation.

"Excuse me," I say, my voice carrying farther than intended in the morning quiet. "I need help. Someone's been hurt, and I can pay for medical supplies."

The conversations stop. Six pairs of eyes turn toward me, assessing the threat level I possess and calculating whether they carry an advantage over me. I'm clean, well-dressed, despite yesterday's chaos. It's obvious I don't belong here.

It's even more obvious that I'm desperate.

"You a cop?" asks a woman with graying hair pulled back in a severe ponytail. Her coat is too big, held closed with duct tape, but her eyes are sharp, intelligent, and miss nothing.

"No." I swallow hard. "My—my friend was shot. We can't go to a hospital. I need someone to buy medical supplies."

"Shot?" A younger man steps forward, maybe mid-thirties, with a scraggly beard and hands that shake slightly. "Why can't you go to a hospital?"

"It's complicated."

"Complicated how?"

The questions come faster now, the group's suspicion shifting toward curiosity. These people understand complicated. They live it every day.

"Bad people are looking for us," I say finally. "Hospital means they find us. My friend dies either way—from the wounds or from them."

The woman with the ponytail—clearly the group's leader—studies my face with the intensity of someone who's learned to read people for survival.

"What kind of supplies?" she asks.

I unfold the list and read it aloud. "Gauze pads, medical tape, antiseptic, ibuprofen, protein bars, water bottles."

"That's maybe twenty-five dollars at the corner store," says a man wearing a military surplus jacket with faded patches. His voice carries the flat precision of someone who's counted every penny for too long. "You said you could pay."

"Fifty dollars." I pull out the bills Cooper gave me, hold them where everyone can see. "Twenty-five for supplies. Twenty-five when they're delivered."

The money changes everything. Backs straighten. Eyes sharpen. Twenty-five dollars is a day's worth of meals, maybe more.

"I'll do it," the young man with the beard says immediately.

"Like hell," snaps someone else. "I was here first."

"You can't even walk to the corner without falling over," the woman says, voice cutting through the argument. She turns to me. "I'll go. But I want the money first."

I extend the bills, and she takes them, counts twice. The paper disappears into her coat pocket.

"Ten minutes," she says. "Corner store's two blocks. I'll be back."

"What if you don't come back?" The question slips out before I can stop it.

She laughs, sharp and bitter. "Honey, if I wanted to steal your money, I'd pick a target who wasn't standing in the middle of my home asking for help." Her expression softens slightly. "Your friend really shot?"

"Yes."

"Bad?"

The image flashes through my mind—Cooper's blood-soaked shirt, the way his hands shook when he thought I wasn't looking, how his voice got rougher as he fought to stay conscious.

"Yes," I whisper.

"Name's Janet." She nods once. "Ten minutes."

And she's gone, walking with purposeful strides toward the street. I stand awkwardly beside the fire, trying not to stare at the people who've witnessed my transaction. The silence stretches until the military jacket man speaks.

"Your friend military?"

"Former."

"Thought so. Only military folks think they can patch bullet holes with T-shirts and willpower."

"Does that usually work?"

"Sometimes. Depends on the holes."

The minutes crawl past. I check my watch obsessively—three minutes, five minutes, seven minutes. What if she doesn't come back? What if the store doesn't have what we need? What if Cooper's bleeding out while I stand here burning precious time on faith and desperation?

Eight minutes. Nine.

At precisely ten minutes, Janet returns carrying a plastic bag. Relief floods through me so intensely that my knees go weak.

"Got everything on your list," she says, handing me the bag. "Plus some extra gauze. Figured you might need it."

I peek inside—white packages of sterile gauze, medical tape, a bottle of hydrogen peroxide, ibuprofen, energy bars, water bottles. Everything Cooper needs.

"Thank you," I breathe. "Thank you so much."

"Hope your friend makes it." She turns to walk away, then pauses. "Next time someone tells you people like us can't be trusted, you remember this."

"I will."

The bag clutches against my chest as I hurry back toward the maintenance shed. The medical supplies inside shift and rustle with each step, a promise of hope wrapped in sterile plastic packaging.

Cooper has to be okay. He has to be.

The shed's door opens to the metallic smell of blood. Cooper sits slumped against the concrete wall, head tilted back, eyes closed. For one terrible moment, I think I'm too late.

Then his chest rises and falls, shallow but steady.

"Cooper?" I whisper.

His eyes open slowly, pupils dilated and unfocused. "You came back."

"Of course I came back." I drop to my knees beside him, setting the bag where he can see it. "Now let me take care of you."

"Eliza—"

"No." The word comes out sharper than intended, carrying all the fear and desperation of the last hour. "You took care of me. Now I take care of you."

For once, he doesn't argue.

I start with the antiseptic, the sharp chemical smell cutting through the concrete mustiness. "This is going to hurt."

"Do it."

The makeshift bandages peel away to reveal wounds that look worse than I remembered. The shoulder entry and exit points are ragged and angry red around the edges. Blood seeps from torn muscle, but it's not the bright arterial spray that would mean we're out of time.

Yet.

"My father always said gunshot wounds were like bad poetry," I murmur, soaking gauze with hydrogen peroxide. "They look dramatic, but most of the damage is internal and hard to see."

"Your father treated gunshot wounds?"

I press the antiseptic-soaked gauze against the entry wound. Cooper's jaw clenches, but he doesn't make a sound. "He said the ones who talked through the pain did better than the ones who suffered in silence."

"Good thing you never shut up."

Despite everything, I almost smile. "Very funny."

The peroxide foams white against the torn tissue, bubbling as it cleans debris from the wound. Cooper's breathing stays controlled, but his hands curl into fists against the concrete floor.

"Tell me about the person," he says through gritted teeth. "The one who got the supplies."

I move to the exit wound, larger and messier. "Her name is Janet. She counted the money twice, told me if she wanted to steal fifty dollars, she'd pick a better target."

"Smart woman."

"She reminded me of my graduate adviser. Same look in her eyes—like she'd seen everything and wasn't impressed by most of it." The antiseptic burns through the wound, and Cooper's breath hisses between his teeth. "Sorry. Almost done with this part."

"Keep talking."

"She said to remember this the next time someone tells me people like her can't be trusted." Clean gauze replaces the blood-soaked fabric Cooper had pressed against the wound. "I think she was making a point about assumptions."

"What kind of assumptions?"

"That homeless means hopeless. That desperation equals dishonesty. That people who have nothing are more likely to take what little you have." I tape the gauze securely, covering both entry and exit wounds with sterile padding. "Academic preju-dices, I guess."

"Not academic. Human." He pauses, studying my face. "Did you tell her that? About believing in humanity?"

"No, she had this look when she counted the money—like she was deciding whether I was worth the risk." I adjust the tape, ensuring the bandage will stay in place. "There was a moment where I thought she might just walk away with the fifty dollars. Not because she's dishonest, but because why should she trust me? I'm some random woman who shows up asking for help, offering money that could be fake or part of some scam."

"But she didn't walk away."

"She didn't walk away. And when she came back, she brought extra gauze. Said she figured we might need it." I move to examine the head wound, dabbing away dried blood with clean gauze. "That's not doing a job for money. That's caring about the outcome."

The ribs require less work—a shallow graze that looks worse than it is. I clean it quickly, apply antiseptic that makes Cooper curse under his breath, then cover it with gauze and tape.

"How do you feel?" I ask, sitting back on my heels.

"Like I got shot."

"But alive?"

"Alive."

I hand him two ibuprofen and a water bottle. "For the pain and inflammation."

He swallows the pills without question, drains half the bottle. Color starts returning to his cheeks, and his breathing deepens.

"Thank you," he says quietly.

"Thank that woman. She's the one who took the risk."

"Thank you for trusting her."

The words hit harder than expected. Trust isn't something that comes easily to either of us—him because of his training, me because of academic competition and professional betrayals. But today I trusted a stranger with Cooper's life, and she proved worthy of that trust.

"I had to," I say. "The alternative was watching you bleed out."

"Still. You did good."

The praise warms me more than it should. Cooper doesn't give compliments lightly, and hearing approval in his voice makes something tight in my chest finally loosen.

SEVENTEEN

Cooper

VULNERABILITY

THE SILENCE STRETCHES BETWEEN US AFTER OUR REALIZATION that Phoenix is becoming part of the system itself. The extraction timeframe feels both too long and not nearly enough—too long to stay hidden from Phoenix's expanding search, not nearly enough time to stop whatever is happening.

My shoulder throbs with each heartbeat—steady, manageable, but a reminder that I'm compromised. The fresh bandages Eliza applied earlier are holding, but blood has seeped through the gauze. Not arterial—I'd be dead already—but enough to keep me weak, slow my reflexes. In a firefight, weakness kills. Right now, sitting in this concrete box with limited escape routes, weakness could kill us both.

The maintenance shed's single bulb casts harsh shadows across Eliza's face as she stares at the laptop screen, processing the implications of what we've discovered. Phoenix isn't hiding anymore—it's integrating and becoming too big to kill without destroying the entire system it now inhabits.

My mental map of the area updates automatically. We're three blocks from the homeless camp where Eliza got supplies.

Phoenix teams swept through here six hours ago—systematic, professional, but they moved on when initial searches turned up nothing. They'll return with expanded parameters, better equipment, and more personnel.

Standard hunter-killer protocol: expand the search radius, increase the team size, and systematically eliminate hiding spots. I've run these operations.

Fast. Efficient. Inevitable.

The shed offers decent concealment but zero tactical advantage. One entrance, no secondary exits, concrete walls that amplify sound. If Phoenix finds us here, we're trapped. My shoulder won't handle sustained combat, and Eliza, for all her newfound competence, isn't a trained operator.

We need better ground. Somewhere with multiple exits, civilians for cover, and infrastructure that complicates their approach. But moving means exposure, and I'm not sure my legs will hold steady under stress.

"Find anything else in the communications?" I ask, shifting against the concrete wall. The movement sends fresh pain through my shoulder, but staying in one position too long creates stiffness that's worse than the discomfort.

"More Phoenix communications. References to something called 'corporate integration Phase Three.' Timeline acceleration due to 'Wren compromise.'" Her fingers pause on the keyboard. "They're moving faster because of what I decoded."

The guilt in her voice cuts through my tactical assessment. She thinks this is her fault. That discovering Phoenix's financial network somehow created the danger instead of revealing it.

"Not your fault," I say. "You uncovered an existing threat. Didn't create it."

She finally looks at me, green eyes searching my face for something—reassurance, maybe, or confirmation that I'm not just saying what she needs to hear.

"Cooper, I need to ask you something, and I need an honest answer."

The serious tone makes my chest tighten. Whatever she's about to ask, it matters to her in ways that go beyond our tactical situation.

"Ask."

"Are you going to die from these wounds?"

Direct. No academic dancing around the subject. She wants a tactical assessment, not comfort.

"No."

"How can you be certain?"

"Blood loss is manageable. The wounds are clean. I've been hurt worse and remained operational."

"When?"

The question catches me off guard. Most people accept medical assessments without demanding case studies. However, Eliza processes information by connecting data points and building understanding through examples.

"Afghanistan. Took shrapnel in three places, walked eight miles through Taliban territory."

"And you survived."

"Obviously."

"Syria?"

She remembers my earlier reference. Her academic brain files away details and cross-references information to build complete pictures.

"Bullet through the thigh. Still completed the mission."

"So these wounds—"

"Are manageable," I finish. "I'm not dying on you."

She closes the laptop and moves closer, close enough that her vanilla scent cuts through the metallic smell of blood and the musty scent of concrete. She touches my forehead, checking for fever.

"You're running warm, but not dangerously so." Her fingers brush across my temple, gentle but sure. "When's the last time you let someone take care of you?"

The question hits harder than expected. When was the last time? Before Syria, maybe, but even then, I was the protector, the one who handled problems, who stayed strong while others needed support. That's what operators do—we take care of others, not the other way around.

"Don't need taking care of."

"That's not what I asked." Her hand moves to my good shoulder, applying steady pressure that makes the pain in the damaged one more bearable. "I asked when it last happened, not whether you needed it."

"Long time."

"How long?"

She's not going to let this go. Her academic persistence is applied to personal questions—the same thoroughness she brings to decoding ancient languages is now focused on decoding me.

"Five years. Maybe six."

"Before your team was killed."

Not a question. She's connecting data points, understanding that losing my team meant more than professional failure. It meant cutting off every connection that made me human instead of just operational.

"Cooper." Her voice drops, becomes softer without losing its certainty. "What happened to them wasn't your fault either."

The words hit. How does she know what I don't want to discuss? How does she find the wounds that never healed and press against them with the ability to not only make me share, but also want to share those pieces of myself with her?

"You don't know what happened."

"No, I don't." Her hand remains steady on my shoulder. "But I know you. And I know you would blame yourself for something that was beyond your control. If it's not too painful, can you share with me what happened?"

"I was overwatch. Sniper position. Watched them walk into an ambush and couldn't do anything to stop it. Too many hostiles, not enough bullets. Had to watch my team die while I tried to pick off targets I couldn't reach fast enough."

"That's not failure, Cooper. That's impossible mathematics." Her voice carries quiet certainty. "One sniper against multiple hostiles—you couldn't have saved them all. No one could have."

She's absolving me of the responsibility I've carried for years, but absolution only works if you believe you deserve it.

"If I'd been better—"

"If you'd been psychic." Her hand tightens on my shoulder. "You're not responsible for information you didn't have. Just like I'm not responsible for Phoenix existing before I found it."

It's parallel reasoning. She's drawing connections between my guilt and hers, showing me how irrational my self-blame is by reflecting it back through her situation.

Smart woman. Too fucking smart.

"Why does it matter to you?" I ask. "Whether I blame myself for old missions?"

"Because." She pauses, as if considering her words carefully. "Because I care about you, and I don't want someone I care about to carry guilt that isn't his to carry."

The simple admission hangs in the air between us. She said it matter-of-factly, the way she might announce a linguistic discovery or tactical observation. No dramatic buildup, no requests for reciprocation. Just truth, offered without conditions.

"Eliza—"

"You don't have to say anything." She reopens the laptop, her fingers moving across the keyboard with renewed focus. "I just needed you to know. In case we don't make it out of this."

In case we don't make it out.

The tactical part of my brain starts calculating survival odds, escape routes, and resource management. But another part—the part that's been dormant since Syria—focuses on the woman beside me, the way she's trying to protect me by not demanding emotional responses I might not be ready to give.

She's giving me space to process. Time to think. The same patience she showed when teaching me that her verbal processing wasn't just chatter, but a methodology.

The silence stretches between us, but it's not uncomfortable. She's learned to read my silences, to understand that I need time to process emotional information the same way she needs to talk through analytical problems.

"We're moving tonight," I say finally. "After midnight, when foot traffic dies down."

"Where?"

"Downtown. Union Station area. More crowds, better transit options, places Phoenix can't control easily."

"Can you walk that far?"

It's an honest question deserving of an honest answer. "If I pace myself. Take breaks. Let you help when I need it."

"Just tell me what you need." No hesitation, no doubt.

What I need. Not what tactical situations require or mission parameters demand. What I, Cooper McKenzie, need from her.

The distinction matters more than it should.

She returns to the decoded Phoenix communications, and I watch her work. The way she processes information, talks through problems, and builds understanding piece by piece. The academic habits that first irritated me now seem like strategic advantages. She thinks out loud because it helps her process. Simple as that.

I lean back against the concrete wall, eyes closing despite the tactical risk. Blood loss creates fatigue that's hard to fight, and her presence beside me creates a sense of security I haven't felt in years. She's watching for threats while I recover. Standing guard while the guardian rests.

She's protecting me.

The irony isn't lost on me. The woman I was hired to keep safe is now the one maintaining security while I deal with injury and exhaustion. But instead of feeling diminished, it feels like a partnership. Like having backup I can trust.

"Cooper." Her voice pulls me back from the edge of sleep. "These Phoenix communications—they reference a specific timeline. 'Phase Three authorization pending until target date.' That's soon."

"What happens then?"

"I don't know, but Phoenix is working toward a deadline." Her fingers move across the keyboard, pulling up more decoded messages. "And whatever they're planning requires corporate infrastructure to be in place first."

The timeline compression makes tactical sense. Phoenix isn't adapting to our discovery—it's accelerating an existing operational plan. Whatever Ashfall represents, whatever Phase Three means, we've forced it to move faster than it wants.

"How much more can you decode before we move?"

"Give me four hours. I can have most of their recent communications analyzed."

"You have three hours. Then we prep for movement."

She nods, accepts the timeline without argument. She understands operational necessities and trusts my tactical judgment, just as I'm learning to trust her analytical expertise.

The pain medication from my go-bag dulls the worst of the shoulder pain, but it also makes thinking harder. My eyelids feel heavy, and staying alert requires conscious effort. But Eliza's presence beside me, her fingers moving across the keyboard, the soft sound of her breathing—it all creates a sense of security that lets my guard down just enough to rest.

Not sleep. Never full sleep in hostile territory. But rest. Recovery. Letting my body heal while she maintains watch.

"Cooper?" Her voice is softer now, careful not to startle me.

"Yeah."

"Thank you. For trusting me to keep watch."

The simple gratitude hits harder than expected. She understands what it means for someone like me to be able to rest while someone else handles security. To show vulnerability instead of strength. To accept help instead of providing it.

"Thank you for earning that trust."

She smiles, returns to her work, and I let my eyes close again, just for a few minutes. Just long enough to allow the painkillers to work and my strength to return.

Outside, the sounds of the city continue—traffic, sirens, the normal rhythms of a place where people live their lives unaware that an artificial intelligence is systematically infiltrating every system that keeps their world functioning.

In three hours, we leave this concrete box and take the fight to Phoenix. But right now, resting while Eliza works, processing her admission that she cares about me, I realize the stakes have changed.

This isn't about stopping Phoenix anymore. It's about surviving long enough to find out what it means that she cares about me.

And whether I'm capable of caring back.

EIGHTEEN

Eliza

NIGHT MOVE

Midnight turns the maintenance shed into a coffin of shadows. The single bulb flickered out an hour ago, leaving only the blue glow of my laptop screen illuminating Cooper's face as he checks his weapon. His jaw clenches with each movement, though he tries to hide the pain.

"Ready?" His voice comes rough and low.

The gun feels wrong in my hands—cold metal against sweaty palms. I grip it like some talisman against the darkness while Cooper drifted in and out of consciousness. Now it's time to move.

"As I'll ever be."

Cooper shoulders the tactical bag with his good arm. Blood has soaked through the bandage again—a dark stain spreading across clean white gauze. The antibiotics from the first aid kit might be keeping infection at bay, but they're doing nothing for the blood loss.

"Stay close," he says, moving to the door. "Voice discipline. Hand signals only unless absolutely necessary."

That's his way of telling me to keep my mouth shut.

My academic brain files away the instructions while my body vibrates with adrenaline. Three hours of decoded Phoenix communications flash behind my eyelids every time I blink—corporate shell companies, financial transfers, systematic infiltration into legitimate businesses. The knowledge weighs heavier than the gun.

Cooper cracks the door open, scanning the darkness beyond. The night air rushes in—cool against my skin, carrying the scent of damp concrete and distant garbage. When he signals all-clear, my feet move automatically.

The alley stretches ahead like a throat, narrowing toward distant streetlights. Cooper moves with measured steps—slower than before, favoring his wounded side. Pride keeps his spine straight, but each footfall betrays the effort it costs him.

"Left at the corner," he whispers. "Stay in the shadows."

I press close to the brick wall, following his lead as we navigate the urban maze. Cooper's tactical training maps our route through blind spots where security cameras can't reach—service corridors, maintenance alleyways, and the forgotten spaces between buildings, where homeless people build cardboard shelters.

The distance to Union Station stretches three miles across a city that never truly sleeps. Every passing car makes my heart stutter. Every distant siren sends ice through my veins. Cooper reads my fear without looking, his hand finding mine in the darkness, squeezing once.

Reassurance without words.

The streets become progressively busier as we approach the edge of the business district. Late-night workers, club-goers, and the occasional group of tourists mix on sidewalks—normal urban nightlife that should provide perfect cover.

Cooper suddenly stiffens beside me, his pace slowing to an almost casual stroll. His hand finds mine, fingers interlacing as he pulls me closer to his side.

"Couple at the bus stop," he murmurs against my hair, lips barely moving. "Man reading newspaper, woman checking phone."

My gaze drifts toward them—nothing remarkable, just two people waiting for public transportation. The man's suit appears slightly rumpled after a long day, while the woman's sensible heels suggest office work.

"What about them?" I whisper back.

"Three things. Positioning gives sight lines in both directions. The newspaper's yesterday's edition. And no bus runs this route after eleven."

The tactical assessment hits like a revelation. What looked like ordinary citizens transforms before my eyes—their casual stance now reads as alertness, their unremarkable appearance as deliberate camouflage.

"Phoenix?"

Cooper's slight nod sends ice through my veins. His grip tightens as he guides me across the street, using a group of laughing twenty-somethings as visual cover.

"More at the corner," he says, eyes scanning the intersection ahead. "Man with coffee cup hasn't taken a sip in three minutes. The woman with the dog is walking too slowly, and there is no plastic bag for waste."

The details blur past my untrained eyes—minor inconsistencies I would never notice become glaring signals to Cooper. He reads the urban landscape like I read linguistic patterns, identifying anomalies that reveal hidden threats.

Cooper guides me toward a narrow alley between buildings. "They're establishing a perimeter from the safe house. Standard procedure—identify an area of interest, place watchers at all exit points, then sweep inward."

"How do you know all this? How can you spot them so quickly?"

A ghost of a smile touches his mouth. "Because it's what I would do."

He pulls me deeper into the alley, away from our planned path. The detour takes us through narrower passages, dirtier corridors where rats scurry away from our approach. Cooper's breathing grows labored, each step heavier than the last.

"Cooper—"

"I'm fine."

The lie hangs between us. Blood seeps through his bandage, leaving a trail any trained operative could follow. His skin has gone ashen in the weak moonlight.

The route becomes a blur of brick walls and concrete floors, service entrances and loading docks. Cooper navigates with certainty despite his condition; sheer determination and force of will carrying him forward when strength fails. My hand stays against his back, offering support he refuses to acknowledge.

When his knees finally buckle, an hour into our journey, I'm there to catch his weight. He sags against me, face pressed into my neck, breath hot against my skin.

"Just need—a minute."

"Take all the time you need."

The abandoned storefront offers temporary shelter—broken windows covered with plywood, the door hanging off rusted hinges. Inside, it smells of old cigarettes and forgotten dreams. Dust swirls around our feet as Cooper slides down the wall, head dropping back against peeling paint.

"How far?" My voice breaks the silence.

"Mile and a half. Maybe two."

His eyes close, lashes dark against pale skin. The bandage needs changing—red has soaked through completely now, tacky and dark in the dim light filtering through cracks in the plywood.

"Let me check your shoulder."

"Later."

"Cooper." My tone drops, becomes commanding in a way that surprises us both. "That's not a request."

Something flickers across his face—respect, maybe, or the simple recognition that stubbornness won't stop blood loss. He unzips the tactical vest with his good hand, allowing me access to the wound.

The bandage peels away with a wet sound that turns my stomach. The entry wound looks angry—red and swollen around the edges, though not yet showing the telltale streaks of infection. Fresh blood wells up as I clean it with supplies from the medical kit.

"Fucking Phoenix," Cooper mutters through gritted teeth as I press a clean bandage against torn flesh. "Turning a simple extraction into this shitshow."

"Simple extraction?" The laugh bubbles up unbidden. "Is that what I was supposed to be?"

His eyes open, finding mine in the darkness. "You were never simple, Eliza."

The words carry weight beyond their syllables. Something shifts between us—acknowledgment of the complexity we've become to each other. More than protector and protected. We defy tactical categories.

His good hand catches mine as I secure the fresh bandage. Fingers curl around my wrist, thumb pressing against my pulse point.

"We need to move."

Phoenix won't stop hunting. The knowledge hangs between

us like inevitability—they have resources, manpower, technology. All we have is Cooper's tactical knowledge and my decoded intelligence. It doesn't feel like enough.

Outside, the city sleeps fitfully under a cloud-smeared sky. Cooper moves more deliberately now, each step calculated to preserve energy. The gun stays ready in his good hand, eyes constantly scanning for threats.

My academic brain tries to process everything—the danger, the mission, the complexity of Phoenix's operation that I've uncovered—a financial web and corporate takeovers. But physical reality keeps intruding—the sharp pain in my feet from miles of walking, the sweat cooling against my skin, the weight of the flash drive pressed between my breasts.

When the train yard appears ahead, Cooper's shoulders relax marginally. The sprawling complex offers cover, multiple routes, and proximity to our destination. Steel tracks gleam dully under security lights, empty train cars lined up like sleeping giants.

"Through there." Cooper points toward a gap in the fence. "Union Station maintenance tunnels connect to the yard. Service entrance will be guarded, but there's a ventilation shaft that bypasses security."

The fence slices my palm as I squeeze through the gap, adding another small pain to the catalog of discomforts. Cooper follows with difficulty, his larger frame struggling through the narrow opening, fresh blood staining his bandage from the effort.

Train yards exist in a different temporal reality—neither fully night nor day, operating on rhythms separate from the city above. Workers move between cars with flashlights, their voices carrying across empty space. We stay low, using the massive wheel assemblies for cover.

Cooper's hand finds the small of my back, guiding me toward a concrete structure squatting between tracks. The maintenance access looks abandoned—rust streaking the metal door, warning signs faded by years of exposure.

"Here."

The lock yields to Cooper's tactical knife, tumblers clicking into place. The door swings open with a groan that makes me wince, revealing stairs descending into darkness.

"Stay close. These tunnels are a maze."

Underground, the air changes—cooler, damper, carrying the metallic scent of machinery and the earthier smell of concrete that never sees sunlight. Our footsteps echo despite careful placement, each sound magnified by curved walls.

"These tunnels run under most of Union Station," Cooper whispers, his voice bouncing back from the darkness ahead. "Maintenance access, electrical conduits, old storage areas from when the station was built."

"How do you know this place?"

"Cerberus ran an operation here three years ago. Arms dealer using passenger luggage to move product."

The casual mention of his past operations creates a strange intimacy—glimpses into the life he lived before Phoenix, before me. Each revelation forms another piece of the puzzle that is Cooper McKenzie.

The tunnel branches, then branches again. Cooper navigates with certainty despite the darkness, one hand trailing along the wall, the other still holding his weapon. When he finally stops, we've reached a junction where several tunnels converge into a larger space.

"Here." He gestures toward a metal door set into the concrete wall. "Maintenance office. Abandoned when they upgraded the systems five years ago."

The room beyond is small but functional—desk pushed against one wall, filing cabinets rusted with age, a cot that must have served some overnight supervisor in years past. The single window has been painted black, preventing light from betraying our position.

"Is it safe?" The question slips out as Cooper secures the door behind us.

"Safe enough." He sinks onto the desk chair, face tight with pain. "Phoenix won't expect us to double back toward the station. They'll expand their search grid outward, not inward."

The space feels secure in ways the maintenance shed never did—thick concrete walls, multiple escape routes through the tunnel system, proximity to crowds that provide anonymity. For the first time in hours, my shoulders relax.

Cooper's gaze catches on something I missed—an old rotary phone sitting on the desk, its beige plastic yellowed with age.

"Landline." His voice carries unexpected relief. "Still connected."

"How can you tell?"

He lifts the receiver, and the soft hum of a dial tone fills the small space. "Old system. Probably maintained for emergency communications. Phoenix monitors cell networks, internet traffic —but old copper wire? Much harder to tap into without physical access."

His fingers dial a number from memory, movements precise despite his obvious pain. The shoulder wound has soaked through his bandage again, dark stain spreading across the fabric.

Cooper's voice changes when the call connects—deeper, more professional. "Whisper. Authentication code Sierra-Echo-Seven-Niner."

A pause as he listens.

"Affirmative. Safe house compromised. Multiple hostiles. Package secure, but we're mobile." Another pause. "Negative. Took fire. Shoulder's hit. Through-and-through, but it's limiting mobility."

My stomach clenches at the clinical description of his wound.

"Limiting mobility" sounds so much less severe than the reality: Cooper struggling to stay conscious, blood soaking through bandages, skin growing paler by the hour.

"Current position?" His eyes meet mine as he listens. "Roger that. Maintenance office beneath Union Station. Access via southern rail yard service tunnels."

Cooper falls silent, listening intently. His jaw tightens at whatever is being said.

"Understood. No assets in proximity." He rubs his forehead, fatigue evident in every line of his body. "Hold for location assessment."

He covers the receiver with his hand. "Ghost has no one who can reach us quickly. He's checking with Guardian HRS, calling in favors."

"What's Guardian HRS?"

"Hostage Rescue Specialists. Allies. Good people." He returns to the call. "Ghost. Still here."

The wait stretches for minutes, silence broken only by Cooper's measured breathing and the ambient sounds of machinery humming beyond the concrete walls. When the voice returns on the line, Cooper straightens slightly.

"Copy that. ETA ten hours. Confirm extraction point?" He listens, nodding. "I know it. Can reach. Medical support confirmed?"

Whatever the answer, it satisfies him. His shoulders relax marginally.

"Understood. Whisper out."

The phone returns to its cradle with a soft click that seems to seal our fate. Ten hours until extraction. Ten hours of hiding, waiting, hoping Phoenix doesn't expand their search parameters to include these underground tunnels.

"Well?" My voice sounds smaller than intended.

"Guardian team is en route. Extraction in ten hours from the

Washington Monument maintenance tunnels." Cooper leans back in the chair, eyes closing briefly. "They're bringing medical support."

"Ten hours." The time frame stretches impossibly ahead. "Can you make it that long?"

His eyes open, finding mine with stubborn determination. "Have to."

NINETEEN

Eliza

SURRENDER

COOPER'S SIMPLE ANSWER CARRIES THE WEIGHT OF BOTH OUR lives. He'll endure because there's no alternative—because my survival depends on his, because mission parameters demand it, because failing isn't an option he'll entertain.

"Let me see your shoulder." I turn to him, determined to do what I can to ease his pain.

This time, he doesn't argue. His tactical vest comes off with difficulty, each movement deliberate as he tries to minimize the strain on his wounded shoulder. When he finally leans back against the chair, exhaustion etches deep lines around his mouth.

I work automatically. The wound looks worse—angrier, the edges puffier than before. Not infected yet, but moving in that direction.

Cooper watches my face as I work, reading every reaction. "How bad?"

"You'll live." The words come out lighter than I feel. "But you're not winning any beauty contests with this shoulder."

His mouth quirks into something almost resembling a smile. "Never cared about pretty."

"No, you care about effective." My fingers smooth a fresh bandage over cleaned skin. "And right now, you're about sixty percent effective."

"Sixty-five."

"Sixty-three, maybe, and that's my final offer."

The absurdity of haggling over his combat effectiveness while hiding from Phoenix operatives in an abandoned maintenance room strikes us both at the same time. Cooper's laughter comes out rough, almost rusty, like he's forgotten how it works.

The sound transforms his face, softening the hard lines of tactical focus into something more human. My hands freeze against his skin, caught by the unexpected vulnerability of that laugh.

"What?" he asks, noticing my stillness.

"Nothing. Just … You rarely laugh."

His eyes hold mine, something shifting in their depths. "Haven't had much reason to."

The simple admission hangs between us. Cooper doesn't speak about emotions—he communicates through action, through protection, through the physical claiming that left me breathless in the safe house. This quiet acknowledgment of joy's absence in his life cuts deeper than expected.

My hands finish their work, securing the fresh bandage with medical tape. When I step back, Cooper captures my wrist, holding me in place.

"Thank you." The words sound dragged from someplace deep and unpracticed. "For this. For the decoding. For not falling apart when most people would have."

Heat floods my cheeks at the unexpected praise. "I'm still breathing because of you."

"We're both still breathing." His grip tightens slightly. "That's what matters."

Something shifts in the space between us. It's not the echo of a train overhead or the distant rumble of city life above the tunnels.

Ten hours until extraction.

My pulse still hammers from the adrenaline of nearly being killed twice in twenty-four hours.

Cooper sits in the battered chair like it was carved from the concrete itself, ribs rising and falling beneath a chest gone taut with tension and pain.

The overhead light flickers, casting sharp shadows across his face and making him look less like a man and more like a relic of war—cut from stone and scar tissue, silent and immovable. Still dangerous.

Still—breathtaking.

Even wounded, he's more alive than anyone I've ever known.

He watches me cross the space. His gaze is calm. Sharp. Unreadable. "What are you doing?"

I hesitate, the question hitting something soft and undefined inside me. My pulse skitters. I shouldn't have come closer. But I couldn't not.

"I don't know," I say, my voice softer than I intended.

And I don't.

Not exactly.

All I know is that the ache inside me hasn't stopped since the safe house. A slow, constant thrum that began the moment he pressed me to the wall and told me to shut up the only way I'd ever dreamed of being silenced. It's grown louder with each step through this underground tunnel, winding itself tighter every time I glance at him and see what he doesn't say.

It's not lust. It's not even comfort.

It's something else entirely—some raw, unspeakable gravity pulling me toward him, one breath at a time.

His eyes narrow. Not in suspicion. In understanding. As if he's decoding me with the same skill he uses to read a threat in the dark. His body doesn't shift. But something in his expression does. A flicker of awareness. A breath of something personal.

He knows.

This isn't seduction.

This is me trying—clumsily, irrationally—to take care of him. A man who doesn't want care. Who probably doesn't even know what to do with it. But I'm here anyway. Because I don't know how to be anywhere else.

He's bleeding. I'm shaking. And somehow, being near him feels like the only right thing left.

His hand lifts to my hip. A touch so light it barely registers, but still—it grounds me.

"You're trying to take care of me," he says, low and rough.

I nod before I think better of it.

His mouth twitches, almost a smile. Not quite. "That's dangerous."

"I don't care," I breathe.

"You should."

He doesn't sound smug. He sounds like he means it. And maybe I should care. About the danger. About the line we crossed. About all the things that will come unraveled if we keep doing this. But none of that matters. Not when I'm looking at him like this, inches from his mouth, fingers aching to reach for him.

My hand lifts on its own. Finds the rough line of his jaw, where stubble has darkened since yesterday. He leans into my palm like it costs him nothing. But I can feel the tension straining beneath his skin. Can feel the heat radiating from his body.

He's not cold.

He's fire, banked and waiting.

"You scared?" he asks.

"Yes."

His thumb brushes my side, a silent tether.

"Of me?"

"No," I say, and the answer is immediate, undeniable. "Of what I want."

The words taste like confession. The kind I never thought I'd speak out loud. But with him, everything feels stripped down. Honest. Exposed.

His eyes change.

They go dark—not cruel, not harsh. Just hungry. That quiet, calculated shift I've only ever seen on the battlefield of his body, when he's about to make a call no one else would dare.

"You know what that tells me?" he says, voice sandpaper and steel.

"What?"

"That you're not here to comfort me anymore."

My stomach drops.

"You're here to be undone."

I don't answer. I can't. My breath is stuck somewhere in my throat, and my knees feel liquid. He watches me absorb the weight of his words, and then he positions me between his legs— slowly, carefully, but with intent. Even injured, he moves like a conqueror. Like the warrior I dreamed of before I ever knew his name.

His hand slides up my spine, from the small of my back to the base of my neck, where his fingers tighten. Not painful. Just— claiming. "Not Cooper," he murmurs, almost to himself.

I blink, confused. But then I see it. See him.

He's not playing a part.

He's becoming it. The gladiator I dreamed up in the dark. The victor, bloody and brutal, walking off the sand to collect his reward.

"Do you remember what you told me?" he murmurs, thumb stroking behind my ear. "Your fantasy?"

I nod, throat dry.

"You didn't say a soldier. You didn't say a protector." His hand curls into my hair, fisting just enough to make me gasp. "You said a champion. The one who fought and bled and won you."

"Yes," I whisper, my voice barely audible. "But that wasn't real."

"You don't think I'm real?"

He's so close now. Heat radiates between us, his breath ghosting over my cheek as he studies every inch of my face. His ribs must be screaming. His shoulder's torn. But you'd never know it from the way he holds himself—imposing, immovable, mine.

"I do," I admit. "It's just—"

"Silence."

The word cracks through the space like a whip.

And my body obeys before my mind catches up.

He's not asking.

He's taking.

And I'm letting him.

Because whatever shame I once tied to that fantasy, whatever fear I thought would stop me from living it—none of it survives under his gaze. Not here. Not now. There is no shame in surrendering to someone who sees you down to the bone and chooses to stay.

His voice drops. Lethal. Quiet.

"You will not serve me fully clothed."

I flinch, already breathless. "We don't have to—"

He tightens his grip in my hair, a sharp tug that steals the end of the sentence.

"Did I stutter?"

I freeze. Not in fear. In recognition.

This is it.

This is the moment I've read about, dreamed about, feared.

The one where it stops being hypothetical and becomes something else entirely. Something elemental. Something sacred.

My hands rise to the hem of my shirt.

They don't shake. Not visibly. But inside, I'm trembling all over.

I undress.

Not seductively. Not slowly. Just—honestly. Shirt. Bra. Jeans. All of it slides to the floor with a whisper that feels deafening.

The cool air brushes against my skin, and for the first time in my life, I am truly naked in front of someone—not because I've taken off my clothes, but because I've laid bare the part of me I've never even looked at too closely.

Cooper hasn't moved.

But his eyes are on me. Not ogling. Not assessing.

Claiming.

I step toward him.

Closer. Closer still. I stand between his legs, heartbeat in my throat, heat pooling between my legs like a confession I can't swallow.

He's still silent.

And the silence speaks louder than any command.

I lower to my knees.

TWENTY

Eliza

HEAT

THE AIR BETWEEN US TIGHTENS, THICK AS A STORM ABOUT TO break. The cold bite of the concrete burns beneath my knees, but I barely feel it. Every nerve in my body is tuned to him. There's no noise but our breathing, and even that feels deliberate, held back.

A stillness that isn't emptiness … It's control. His control.

I expected him to smirk. To tease. But he doesn't. He just stares at me with an intensity so unflinching it feels like pressure, like weight pressing down over every inch of my exposed skin.

When he finally moves, it's only to cup the side of my face. His thumb brushes my cheekbone, then drifts lower to rest at the hinge of my jaw, like he's testing the muscle. His touch is firm, sure, but not cruel. His fingers trace the shape of my mouth, and I know he's not admiring it. He's owning it.

"You sure?" he asks, voice low and rough, but not uncertain. It's not a question born of hesitation. It's respect. A final pause before everything changes.

I nod. My throat's too tight to speak.

He unbuttons his pants, the sound barely more than a whisper. He frees himself with one hand, and there's no show to it. He's not performing. Not trying to be the fantasy I shared in the dark. He's just being Cooper. And that, somehow, is more intimate than any fantasy I could have conjured.

"Open your mouth."

The command doesn't startle me. It doesn't even feel like a command. It feels like an invitation. My lips part, and I look up at him—not seeking approval.

Just—present.

Completely, wholly present.

He steps forward, the head of his cock brushing against my tongue. The weight of him is immediate. He doesn't thrust. Not yet. He just rests there. Heavy. Warm. Real. I close my lips around him slowly, and his exhale is quiet and ragged, like I've taken more from him than he expected.

His fingers tighten in my hair. Not to pull. To guide.

And when he moves—slow, shallow thrusts—I let go. I let my mind still. Let sensation take the place of shame. Let want replace fear. I've spent my entire life defining myself by words. But right now, there are none. Just the sound of his breath. The soft, wet slide of his body in my mouth. The dizzying ache of surrender.

He doesn't talk much—not the way I do. But now, every quiet sound he makes is a language. A story I understand on instinct. His grunt when I take him deeper. His sharp inhale when my tongue traces the underside. The low curse when I gag, just a little, and don't pull back.

"Just like that," he says, voice cracking with restraint. "Don't you dare stop."

The words don't humiliate me. They anchor me. I'm not ashamed. I'm not small. I'm his. And he's not degrading me—he's recognizing me. Recognizing every hidden part of me I thought I'd buried too deep to ever unearth again.

When he finally pulls free, I'm breathless, dizzy, spit-wet, and aching. But I don't want to stop.

I want all of him.

He hauls me to my feet, slow and careful but without asking, without breaking the thread of dominance that now connects us. My legs tremble. Not from fear. From release. From the space that's opened between us, carved by the heat of his gaze and the softness of his grip.

He turns me—hands on my hips—and bends me over the back of the metal chair. The chill of it shocks my skin, makes me gasp. And still, he doesn't speak. Doesn't ask.

He slides a hand between my thighs, fingers brushing the heat there, the slick evidence of what we've already done. "Fuck," he mutters, low and reverent. "You're dripping."

I bite my lip. Not out of shame. Out of the unbearable truth of how badly I need what comes next.

When he presses inside, it's not brutal.

It's not gentle either.

It's complete.

A slow, steady claiming that fills every inch of me until I'm stretched around him, held open and helpless, right where I need to be. His hand curls around the back of my neck, holding me down—not to dominate, but to center me. To hold me still so I can feel every inch of him. His body. His weight. His need.

He thrusts again. Deeper. My body rises to meet him without thought.

"You think this is a fantasy?" he says, voice gravel and grit and heat. "Think again, Eliza."

I moan, high and broken.

He drives into me without apology, without hesitation, his grip iron at my hips, keeping me braced and open for every brutal, claiming thrust. There's nothing calculated or cautious in the way he moves—just raw male force, anchored by a will honed through combat and silence and years of never needing anyone. Until now.

Until me.

He fucks like he bleeds—without complaint. Without fear. Like the pain in his shoulder doesn't matter. Like the whole goddamn tunnel could collapse around us and he wouldn't stop until I was wrung dry, aching and soaked in the truth of what he does to me.

He pounds deeper, hips slamming into the curve of my ass as I cry out, high and wrecked. My thighs shake. My jaw clenches. I want to crawl away from the overwhelming flood of sensation, and I want to crawl back to him at the same time. He leaves no room for thought, no room for control, just the relentless rhythm of a man using me the way I begged to be used—without permission. Without mercy.

"You feel that?" he growls, his breath hot against the nape of my neck. "This is what happens when you let a man like me in. I don't stop until you can't fucking walk."

His fingers slide between my thighs. Find my clit. And the cry that tears from me is nearly animalistic, my body locking around him as he drags me toward another climax—not tender, not sweet, but brutal and full-bodied and earned.

"You're mine now," he snarls, and I swear I can feel it in my bones. "Not because I said so. Because your body fucking decided."

He fucks me through it, doesn't let me come down, not even for breath. His rhythm is unforgiving, deep and ruthless and perfect. Every thrust is an answer to a question I didn't know I was asking. Every snap of his hips says, this is who I am, and I believe it. I believe him.

I brace against the chair, my voice gone, my body raw, and still I want more. Still, I push back into him like I need to be wrecked to be made whole again.

And when I come—again—it's not an orgasm. It's annihilation. A total obliteration of thought, of time, of the line between fantasy and reality. My body convulses, wrung out and taken. Not held. Not coddled. Claimed.

He follows with a roar that feels more like a release of war than of pleasure, his hands branding my hips as he buries himself one final time and spills inside me.

We don't move.

Can't.

The only sound is the echo of our breathing and the hollow hum of the tunnel lights above, flickering with their own warning rhythm.

He's still inside me when he lowers his forehead to my back, his weight draping over me, solid and trembling. Not from weakness. From restraint. The kind it takes to hold back everything he could've done—and didn't.

And that, more than anything, undoes me.

Because he could've destroyed me.

But he didn't.

He gave me exactly what I asked for.

What I've always needed.

And for the first time, I understand the difference between being used—and being wanted.

We stay like that—pressed together, limbs tangled, breath shallow in the heavy silence of the room. His chest is damp against my back, each exhale a hard-won drag of air. The concrete floor beneath my knees is unforgiving, my thighs tremble from strain, and I'm still slick and open where he left me —taken and held in a way that feels, not undone exactly, but rewritten.

His cock softens inside me, then slips free, and I nearly flinch at the loss. He exhales roughly, the sound more animal than man, and I feel the effort in his body as he straightens, already bracing against the pain his shoulder must be screaming.

He doesn't speak. Just lets his hand slide over my lower back, then up to my spine, steady and grounding. I start to turn toward him, but he beats me to it—gently drawing me upright, his hand still firm at my waist. My legs feel wobbly, my skin flushed, clothes scattered on the floor behind me.

"Get dressed," he murmurs, voice low and frayed at the edges. "You'll freeze."

The words land like a snap of cold air across my skin. Not unkind. Just real. Just Cooper. Practical. Protecting me in the only ways he knows how.

I nod, cheeks hot, and turn to gather my clothes. My hands tremble a little, not from embarrassment, but from the echo of what we just did—the force of it still humming through every nerve. I pull my shirt over my head, tug on my underwear, my jeans. He watches without comment, his gaze steady but unreadable. Not possessive. Not soft. Just there.

When I finish dressing, he moves. Carefully, with a wince and a hiss that tells me how much more pain he's in than he's letting on. His bare chest is still streaked with sweat and dried blood, the makeshift bandage on his shoulder darkening at the edge. He's holding himself stiff, but his eyes never leave me.

"Come here," he says.

It's not a command this time. Not a test or a game.

It's an offer.

I go.

He draws me toward the cot tucked in the corner of the room—thin mattress, threadbare blanket, but it's better than concrete. He sits first, jaw tight with effort, then pulls me gently into his lap, shifting us both down until we're lying across it, my body tucked against his good side. His breath is ragged. His shoulder must be screaming. But he doesn't make me sleep alone.

"You've got nine hours," he murmurs, voice low near my temple. "Before extraction. Maybe less if we're unlucky. Either way—we rest now."

I nod, my fingers curling lightly against his side, over the bruised ribs I know he's ignoring. I want to ask him what all this meant. What we are now. What comes next.

But none of it matters here.

Not in this abandoned room. Not between a woman who finally said her fantasy aloud and the man who answered it without blinking.

His hand finds my back. Just rests there. Warm. Protective. A silent vow.

And as my eyes drift closed, exhaustion finally overtaking adrenaline, I feel it settle inside me—not fear. Not regret.

But this quiet, impossible thing I don't have a name for.

Maybe later, when we're safe, I'll find the words.

But for now, there's nothing left to do but sleep.

And trust that when I wake, he'll still be alive.

TWENTY-ONE

Cooper

EXTRACTION

Eliza sleeps like it costs her everything.

Pressed tight to my uninjured side, breathing slow and even, cheek tucked against my chest like she trusts me to keep the world from caving in. Maybe I do. Maybe that's what's been happening since the second I laid eyes on her—this slow, tectonic shift from detached protector to something else entirely.

Her body still carries the heat of what we did. I can feel the echo of it in the air between us. In the way her hand curls into the hem of my shirt like she won't let go.

I don't want her to.

God help me, I don't want her to let go.

I used to think sex was best kept clean. Quick. Equal pleasure and no promises. No names. No numbers. Just relief, then silence.

But this?

This isn't relief.

It's a detonation.

And now I'm lying here with a woman tucked against my ribs, her scent all over my skin, her breath stirring against my chest—and I'm not restless. I'm not counting the minutes until I can slip out. I'm just here. And for the first time in years, that feels like enough.

Sleep doesn't come easily. Not ever. I drift, but never fall. Constantly aware of the dark. The weight of silence. The feel of pressure shifting when someone enters a room. It's what kept me alive in war zones and alleyways. What's kept me breathing long after I probably shouldn't be alive.

It's that same instinct that jolts me now.

The air changes. A subtle tension. Like a held breath in the concrete bones of the tunnel. My body reacts before my brain finishes catching up. I'm already sitting up, gun in hand, heart picking up speed. A whisper of motion—too far to hear but close enough to know.

I lean over her. "Eliza."

She stirs, lashes fluttering, eyes hazy. "What?"

"We've got to move. Now."

The tone of my voice must hit home because she bolts upright, tension snapping through her limbs as she grabs her shoes. I toss her the go-bag.

"The drive. You got it?"

"Yes."

"Good. On your feet."

I shoulder open the rusted exit door, pistol raised, and we slip back into the arteries of the city's underbelly. The tunnels yawn ahead, damp and echoing. Stale air mixes with the stench of mold and sewage, heavy enough to taste. Water drips from overhead. Pipes hiss. Rats skitter across our path, their claws a rapid, clicking percussion.

One darts too close and Eliza startles with a squeal—high, sharp, unmistakably human. My hand flies up instinctively, pressing firmly against her shoulder, urging her back against the tunnel wall.

"Shhh," I hiss, cutting a look over my shoulder.

She clamps her mouth shut, cheeks flushed with embarrassment. But her breathing's fast and shaky, and when I reach for her hand, she doesn't hesitate. Fingers tighten around mine. I pull her close, tuck her behind me again, and keep moving.

The darkness stretches ahead—uneven concrete, rusted rebar, old signage half-obscured by time and graffiti. These tunnels were never meant for people, not really. Just maintenance crews and ghosts.

We move fast, boots slapping against wet concrete. I keep her tucked behind me, my good hand on her arm, guiding. We round a corner, and a man lunges out of the shadows like he's been waiting for us.

Hunched. Twitching.

Filthy hoodie pulled tight over his head, the glint of a blade trembling in his hand. His eyes are wild, yellowed with fever or something worse, pupils blown wide. The stench hits before his voice does.

"Give me your bag!"

He's strung out, desperate. I can see it in the way his hand shakes around the hilt of the blade, the way his whole body jitters like a live wire. This isn't a mugging. It's a last-ditch gamble for survival.

But I don't hesitate. Can't.

One step forward—my foot snaps low, fast, sweeping his legs from under him. He hits the ground with a wet grunt. The knife clatters from his grip, skittering into the dark. Before he can scramble for it, I'm on him—boot pressed to his chest, pinning him to the slick concrete, his breath wheezing through cracked lips.

"Don't," I warn, voice low and lethal. "Stay the fuck down."

He nods frantically, coughing, palms up. I hold him there just long enough to make sure he's not stupid enough to follow.

Then I kick him hard to the side. He crumples against the wall, groaning.

Not dead. Just out of the way.

I spin, grab Eliza's hand. Her eyes are wide, her body stiff, but she moves when I pull. Around another corner. Down another dark tunnel. The walls close in tighter here. The ceiling is low. Pipes snake overhead like metal veins. The smell intensifies—something rotting in the far recesses.

She slips. A sharp cry. I catch her by the arm, wrench her upright.

White-hot agony tears through my shoulder like lightning laced with glass. The burn isn't just pain. It's a detonation of sensation. Blinding. Crippling. My knees nearly buckle. The bandage beneath my jacket goes hot and wet.

Fuck.

The wound is open again.

Blood surges down my arm, soaking through fabric that's already stiff with dried sweat and old crimson. I grit my teeth so hard my jaw creaks, vision narrowing to a tunnel of pulsing red.

"Shit," I bite out, barely managing to keep her upright as my legs scream to fold.

"You're bleeding again," she gasps, reaching for me.

"I'll live," I growl, but my voice is hoarse, thinner than I want. "Keep moving."

She doesn't argue. Just runs.

The tunnel opens into a broader artery beneath the city, where the dim flicker of dying fluorescent fixtures sputters overhead, casting sickly pools of light that barely touch the filth below. A rusted barrel burning at the far end throws orange shadows against damp, mildew-stained concrete. The acrid stink of smoke mingles with the ammonia burn of piss, the sour reek of sweat, rot, and days-old vomit. The air is thick—wet with decay and city waste, a place where sunlight has never reached.

Boxes, blankets, tarps strung up with scavenged wire—makeshift shelters for the forgotten. Homeless people line the edges like ghosts in tattered layers, but this is no passive gauntlet—we're running a razor's edge through it.

One man stirs, eyes bleary and bloodshot, face streaked with soot. Another, bundled beneath a shredded sleeping bag, rocks in place, muttering nonsense prayers to the flickering ceiling. And then a third erupts from a nest of garbage bags, red-rimmed eyes sharp with fury, a broken bottle clenched in his hand like a weapon.

"Fuck you doing down here?"

"Move," I growl.

He doesn't. Not right away.

I shoulder into him hard, not slowing, not stopping. My shoulder screams, more blood spills, dripping down my arm, but I grit my teeth and shove him aside. He stumbles, crashes into a wall of milk crates, cursing. Another man lunges out of a tent—filthy beard, wired eyes, arms outstretched like he's going to stop us. I twist at the last second, drive my elbow into his gut. He folds. Wheezing.

Eliza gasps. Someone grabs at her arm. I whirl—pistol raised, safety off. The shadow disappears back into the dark, muttering.

"Keep going." I shove her ahead.

Around us, the camp rouses like a kicked hornet's nest. People shout and curse, darting from makeshift shelters and tarp-covered beds. A tent collapses beneath someone's weight, spilling its contents and tangled limbs into the muck. A bottle shatters underfoot, glinting fire-orange in the flickering glow of the barrel nearby.

Screams rip through the smoke-choked air. We've told every goddamn gunman chasing us exactly where to go. We've brought them down on our heels.

Behind us, booted feet hammer the concrete. They're

coming. Not just one or two now. More. Gaining ground with every breath. Every limp I can't hide.

The tunnel narrows again ahead, sloping into another turn. Slick. Cramped. We plunge forward, the corridor pressing in, breath hot in our chests. My shoulder pulses like it's being torn apart from the inside out.

And still, I run. Eliza stumbles, her breathing ragged, sharp. Fear vibrates off her skin like static.

Behind us, the sound we've been running from grows louder—booted feet stomping over the ground, the distant crash of metal, something kicked or knocked aside.

Close. Too close.

A shadow separates from the wall. Another druggie. Another broken life.

"Move," I growl, my voice flint and fire.

But he doesn't.

He's in the way. And we don't have time.

I twist, shoving Eliza behind me, and slam my shoulder into him, the wrong one. Agony rips through me like shrapnel. Wet heat spreads down my arm. The bandage is gone, torn loose. I bite down on the yell trying to claw its way up my throat.

But the bastard stumbles. That's all I need.

I push Eliza past him, my hand gripping hers tight. Her breath comes fast, shallow—the high, whimpering edge of terror slipping through her clenched teeth.

Behind us, chaos erupts. The homeless camp boils to life with shouts, questions, curses—and footsteps. Fast. Heavy. Drawing closer.

They're closing in fast.

Behind us, the sound we've been outrunning gets louder. Boots. At least three. Maybe more. The shuffle of movement. The clang of something metal knocked over.

We pick up speed, cutting through the camp. Shouts rise behind us.

"They went that way!"

"Hey! Who the hell—"

Gunfire cracks. A burst of panic erupts from the camp. Screams. People running.

We round another corner. My lungs burn. Every nerve is on fire. My shoulder pulses like a detonator. The tunnel opens wide here. Too wide.

I shove her into cover behind a crumbling concrete support. "They're on us."

"How many?"

I glance back. One. Two. Three shadows gaining ground. More behind them. My grip tightens around the pistol. "More than I've got bullets."

Eliza's eyes go wide. Her breath stutters, panic blooming on her face. I step out just enough to draw a clean line of sight and squeeze off the first shot.

Crack. The lead man drops.

Second shot—center mass. The next crumples sideways, gasping.

Third. Fourth. Fifth—each round precise, honed. The last man lurches forward before crashing into the filth, a wet grunt his only epitaph.

And then—I'm dry.

My thumb taps the empty slide reflexively. "Out."

I turn toward Eliza, body tensed, ready to shield her with whatever I have left. Suddenly, gunfire shatters the darkness.

I grab her, press her hard to the tunnel wall, my body caging hers, expecting death from both directions.

But the shots land behind us.

Men scream. Footsteps scatter. Someone goes down hard.

Then—voices. Clear. Clipped. Commanding.

"Cerberus! Lower your weapon!"

I look up.

Tactical black. No insignia. No names. Helmets pulled low. Rifles braced high.

Guardians.

A rifle clatters through the air. I catch it one-handed, already pivoting.

"You're late," I say, panting, blood slick down my arm, breath catching on the edges of pain.

"Get to the extraction point." The Guardian doesn't blink. His voice is gravel and steel behind the visor. "We'll hold the line. Get her to safety. We've got this."

He slides past me, already firing, movements lethal and fluid. Another figure materializes beside him, covering our flank.

I nod once, grab Eliza's hand, and pull her forward. And for the first time in days, it feels like we might actually make it out alive.

TWENTY-TWO

Eliza

BENEATH THE SURFACE

THE STINK OF BURNT GUNPOWDER AND COOPER'S BLOOD FILLS MY nostrils as we stumble through the dim tunnels. Gunfire echoes behind us, each shot a reminder of how close death follows. Cooper's grip on my hand weakens with every step, his breathing becoming more labored. My mind races between the data we've uncovered, the extraction coordinates, and the terrifying possibility that Cooper might not make it.

"Almost there," Cooper grunts, his voice rough with pain. "Junction ahead."

The tunnel widens into a concrete chamber marked with faint chalk symbols that would be invisible to anyone who didn't know to look for them. In the weak emergency lighting, I can just make out three silhouettes waiting in tactical formation— Guardian operatives in black gear, faces obscured, moving with the precision that speaks of years of operational experience.

No words are exchanged. No introductions. Just a quiet command from the tallest figure: "Up. Now."

A telescoping ladder drops from a shaft above, extending

down with a metallic hiss. I stare up into darkness; my heart hammering against my ribs.

"You first," Cooper says, his voice barely audible. His face is ashen, sweat beading on his forehead despite the tunnel's chill. "I'll follow."

My hands shake as I grab the first rung. The ladder is slick with grime and moisture, each step up a test of nerves more than strength. My muscles burn with exhaustion, protesting every movement. Below me, Cooper waits, swaying slightly, one hand pressed against his blood-soaked shoulder.

When I reach the top, two gloved hands seize my wrists, pulling me swiftly through the circular opening. I stumble as my feet hit solid flooring, disoriented by the sudden transition from vertical to horizontal movement.

"Easy," a male voice says, steadying me with a firm grip on my elbow.

I blink, adjusting to the dim interior. It's not a street opening as I expected, but a customized tactical van. Red-filtered lights cast everything in a bloody glow, revealing equipment racks along both walls and a central gurney with restraints. The space is tight —maybe fifteen feet long and seven feet wide—with four people in dark tactical gear positioned strategically around the confined area. The air smells of antiseptic, metal, and the coppery tang of blood.

A woman with long brown hair tied in a practical bun guides me to a jump seat bolted to the side wall. Despite the tension in the air, her face has a natural kindness to it, softening her otherwise all-business demeanor. "Sit here. Stay clear of the medical team," she instructs, her voice clipped but gentle. She points to a handhold on the wall next to me. "Use this when we move. It'll get bumpy."

She turns back to the opening in the floor, leaving me perched on the edge of the seat.

"Cooper," I call down, gripping the metal handhold. "Come on."

I watch in horror as he struggles up the ladder, each movement clearly agony. Halfway up, his grip slips, and only the quick reaction of one of the Guardian operatives prevents him from falling. Cooper fights to continue climbing, his face contorted with pain.

Just as he reaches the final rungs, his strength gives out. He lurches forward, collapsing half-in and half-out of the van's opening, blood spreading across his shirt in an alarming pattern.

"Cooper!" I scream, lunging toward him, but strong hands guide me firmly back to my seat.

"Let them work," a low voice orders.

The van's interior is cramped but organized. Four medical professionals in dark tactical gear are positioned around a central gurney, equipment cases stacked against the walls. They spring into action the moment Cooper appears, two of them pulling him fully inside while the others snap open cases of medical supplies and ready IV bags.

"I'm Doc Summers, you can call me Skye," says the woman with the brown hair, her kind eyes briefly meeting mine before returning to Cooper. She assesses his wounds with quick, practiced movements, then looks up sharply at her team. "He's crashing. Let's move."

The team leaps into action. A tall woman with copper skin and nimble fingers tears open Cooper's shirt, revealing the full extent of his injuries. She finds veins in his arms, sliding in two IV catheters with remarkable speed while calling for fluids.

A man who could be Cooper's cousin—same chiseled features, same intensity in his eyes—attaches monitoring leads to Cooper's chest. "Pulse 130 and thready," he reports, reaching for an oxygen mask. "O2 sats 82 and dropping. Starting supplemental."

"Tia, push a unit of plasma," Skye orders, applying pressure to Cooper's side wound. "Ryker, get that portable ultrasound ready. I need to see what we're dealing with."

While the medical team works, a commanding figure with a communications headset turns his attention to me. "CJ, Guardian Team Leader," he says, his voice calm despite the chaos around him. "The woman saving your friend is Dr. Skye Summers. The tall one is Tia, our nurse anesthetist. The guy with the oxygen is Ryker, respiratory technician."

From the shadows steps a man whose presence fills the confined space—tall, with hard eyes that miss nothing. "Mason Blackwood," he says, extending a hand. "Call sign Ghost. Cooper's team leader at Cerberus." His grip is firm but not crushing. "You did good getting him this far. Now sit back and let these people work."

I gasp at the full extent of his wounds—not just the shoulder injury I'd been treating but a second wound along his side that's pumping blood at an alarming rate. The floor of the van is slick with it, bright red against steel gray.

"He's losing too fast," Skye says, her voice cutting through the methodical beeps of monitoring equipment. "Tia, hang two units and push it wide open. Pressure dressing on this lateral wound."

Tia reaches into a refrigerated case, pulling out blood bags. "Blood's cold. Running it through the warmer," she reports, connecting the tubing to a rapid infuser that will both warm the blood and push it in under pressure.

My vision tunnels, the edges going dark as I watch Cooper's life spilling onto the van floor while they race to replace what he's losing. I grip an overhead bar to stay upright, my knuckles white with the effort.

Tia notices, her eyes meeting mine briefly even as she manages the blood transfusion. "It looks worse than it is," she says, her voice steady as she works. "You got him here in time."

The van lurches into motion, tires squealing against pavement. CJ moves to stand beside me, keeping his balance effortlessly as the vehicle weaves through what must be side streets.

"We've been tracking Phoenix's kill squad through the metro system," he explains, his voice low. "Had to neutralize two other teams converging on your position. This van has EM shielding and infrared suppression—you're off their surveillance grid now."

"Off the map," Ghost adds from where he stands watching the medical team work. "You and the drive."

My hand instinctively checks my bra where the flash drive remains secure. All of this—Cooper's blood, the gunfire, the frantic escape—all for the data that could bring down Phoenix.

I stare at the side wound, the one I never treated, never even knew about. He must have been hit again during our mad dash through the tunnels—taking a bullet without telling me, pushing forward despite the new injury. The realization twists my heart. While I was focused on our escape, he was bleeding out from a wound I didn't even know existed.

"Will he …" I can't finish the question.

"Skye's the best," CJ answers. "But he needs surgery. We're heading to our airstrip now."

I nod, unable to form words as Cooper's vital signs flash on the portable monitor. His blood pressure is dangerously low, his oxygen saturation falling despite the mask over his face. Skye presses gauze packs against the wound while Tia pushes medications through the IVs, calling out drug names and dosages in medical shorthand that sounds like a foreign language.

I want to touch him, to whisper that I'm here, that he kept his promise to get me out alive. But he's unconscious, pale as death, sweat beading on his forehead. My mind replays our time together in flashes—the maintenance room, his hands on my body, the way he made me feel safe even when the world was falling apart around us.

Now this. The guilt crashes over me in waves. If I hadn't decoded Phoenix's data, if I hadn't insisted on taking the flash drive, if I had just stayed in my academic bubble—Cooper wouldn't be fighting for his life.

The van weaves through side streets, avoiding main thoroughfares where Phoenix might have surveillance. Through the small window separating the driver's compartment, I glimpse the early morning darkness giving way to predawn gray. We've been running for hours, though it feels like days.

When we finally slow, it's inside a hangar, the van doors opening directly into the cavernous space. A sleek aircraft waits, its engines already humming with readiness. Everything happens with intense coordination—Cooper is transferred to a stretcher, his body covered under the sheets. A mask is placed over my face, matching those worn by the Guardian team.

"Security protocol," Ghost explains as he guides me toward the aircraft. "Even our allies don't know who you are."

The plane is unlike anything I've seen before—clearly military in origin, but retrofitted with medical equipment that rivals any emergency room. We're barely on board before the aircraft begins taxiing, no lights, no radio chatter, just the hum of engines accelerating to takeoff speed.

Inside, the medical team transitions Cooper to a more sophisticated setup. A new face joins them—a man with silver-streaked hair.

"Dr. Asa Khan," Skye introduces him briefly. "Best trauma surgeon in the world."

I'm guided to a seat and buckled in, but I can't tear my eyes away from Cooper. The medical team surrounds him—Skye barking orders while hanging blood products, Tia calling out medications, Ryker reading out vital signs every thirty seconds, and Dr. Khan arranging surgical instruments on a sterile field with the focus of a chess master planning three moves ahead.

When they intubate Cooper, I finally break. The sight of him, my protector, my anchor through this nightmare, now breathing only because a machine forces air into his lungs, shatters something inside me. A sob escapes before I can stop it.

CJ slides into the seat beside me. "This is what we do," he says, his voice surprisingly gentle for a man who looks like he could snap necks with his bare hands. "You saved him. Now let us take over."

The flight passes in a blur of medical procedures and hushed conversations. I drift in and out, exhaustion claiming me in patches, only to jerk awake at every change in Cooper's monitor sounds. When I wake fully, light streams through the small aircraft windows. Below us stretch the jagged peaks of mountains, bathed in the golden glow of sunrise.

"Cascades," Ghost says, noticing my gaze. "We're approaching Seattle."

Cooper lies still on the medical gurney, but his monitors beep with a stronger, steadier rhythm. The breathing tube has been removed, replaced with a nasal cannula. Color has returned to his face—not much, but enough to suggest he's fighting his way back.

As the aircraft begins its descent, Skye approaches, her surgical cap removed, revealing her long brown hair now damp with sweat and coming loose from its bun. Despite the exhaustion evident in the shadows under her eyes, that natural kindness remains in her expression.

"He's stable," she says, her voice reflecting the exhaustion of hours of intensive care. "The surgery went well. The bullet in his shoulder missed the major vessels—your field care helped with that. The side wound was trickier, but we got it under control."

Relief floods through me so intensely that for a moment I can't speak. I just nod, blinking back tears.

The aircraft touches down with barely a bump, taxiing directly into another hangar. When the back hatch opens, the fresh scent of pine and ocean air rushes in, so different from the recycled oxygen and antiseptic smell inside.

Ghost appears beside me as the medical team prepares to move Cooper. "Welcome to Cerberus," he says, his normally hard expression relaxed into something almost approachable. "Phoenix can't reach you here."

Skye gives me a reassuring nod as she checks Cooper's vitals one more time. "He's in good hands," she says quietly. "Both of you are."

As they wheel Cooper out, I follow on shaky legs, the flash drive still secure against my heart. We made it. Against impossible odds, we survived. But as I step into the hangar and see the small army of operatives waiting for us, I realize the fight is far from over.

TWENTY-THREE

Cooper

BROTHERS IN ARMS

The ceiling above me is warm, honey-colored wood—
exposed beams that speak of craftsmanship. My shoulder throbs
with each heartbeat—steady but manageable, and wrapped in
enough gauze to stop a freight train. The other wound pulls
differently in my abdomen—deeper, with surgical tape and
drainage tubes that I don't remember earning.

Must have taken another hit during the tunnel chase.

Adrenaline masks a lot of damage in the moment, but the
body keeps score. The IV in my left arm pulls slightly when I
shift, clear fluid dripping from a bag suspended above my head.
Morphine, probably. Enough to dull the edge but not enough to
compromise my awareness.

Still alive. That's something.

This isn't what I expected to wake up to. No institutional
green walls or fluorescent lighting humming its eternal electric
song. Instead, floor-to-ceiling windows frame a view of snow-
capped peaks that stretch beyond the horizon. The bed beneath
me feels like it belongs in a five-star resort—memory foam and
Egyptian cotton instead of military-issue linens. The room smells

of cedar and fresh mountain air filtering through what must be a high-end ventilation system.

Where the hell am I?

My mental inventory runs automatically: my shoulder is immobilized but functional, my ribs are sore but not broken, my legs are responding to commands, and my fingers are flexing around phantom weapons. The body armor saved me from worse damage, but the blood loss nearly finished what Phoenix started.

Eliza.

Did she make it out? Yes—I remember watching her climb that telescoping ladder, the way Guardian operatives hauled her up into the van with swift, coordinated movements.

She is safe.

The extraction comes back in fragments—my own climb up that ladder, how my arms shook with each rung, the way everything hurt by the time I reached the top. Then the van's red interior lighting, medical equipment that belonged in an emergency room spread throughout what looked like a converted ambulance, only bigger. Everything after the tunnel firefight blurs into pain and darkness.

The door opens with a soft click of quality hardware. Ghost enters first, his imposing frame filling the doorway, followed by the familiar bulk of Halo, who trails behind. Both men move with the confidence of operators in their own territory, but I catch tension around Ghost's eyes—the kind that means debriefings and damage assessments are waiting.

"About time you rejoined the living," Halo says, settling into the chair beside my bed with a grin that doesn't quite hide his relief. "Had us worried there for a minute."

"Takes more than a couple of bullets to put me down." My voice comes out rougher than expected, throat dry from whatever they used to keep me under during surgery. "Eliza?"

"Safe," Ghost answers immediately, understanding the priority. "Guardian HRS extracted both of you clean. Phoenix lost the trail."

The tension in my chest eases for the first time since I regained consciousness. She made it. The mission parameters were satisfied—principal extracted alive.

Threat neutralized.

Objective completed.

So why does relief feel incomplete?

"Package secure?" I ask, falling back on operational terminology because it's easier than admitting personal investment.

Ghost's expression shifts slightly—not disapproval, but recognition. He's been reading people long enough to know when tactical concern crosses into something more personal.

"Package is more than secure," he says, pulling up a second chair. "She's been working with Guardian HRS's technical team for the past eighteen hours. What she decoded ..." He pauses, choosing words carefully. "Changes everything."

Halo leans forward, elbows on his knees. "Your professor cracked something big. Bigger than we thought when we sent you in."

The door opens again, admitting Jackson and the rest of the team. Fuse looks like he hasn't slept—dark circles under his eyes, tactical vest still in place like he came straight from another operation. The concerned expressions around the room tell me more about my condition than any medical chart.

"Jesus, Whisper," Fuse says, taking in the bandages and IV setup. "You look like you went ten rounds with a meat grinder."

"Should see the other guys." The old joke falls flat, but it's what they expect—proof that whatever happened didn't break anything essential.

"What's the count?" Ghost asks, settling into command mode.

"Nine confirmed down during the safe house breach. Three more in the tunnel system during extraction." The numbers come easily, muscle memory cataloging threats eliminated versus ammunition expended. "Phoenix tactical teams. Professional work, but they underestimated urban warfare complications."

"Good shooting," Martinez observes. "Especially considering you were leaking like a sieve."

"Had help." The admission surprises me—acknowledging assistance isn't standard operating procedure, but Eliza deserves credit for keeping me functional long enough to complete the mission. "She handled field medicine better than most trained operators."

Something passes between Ghost and Halo—a look that suggests they've already discussed Dr. Eliza Wren's performance under pressure.

"Speaking of which," Ghost says, rising from his chair, "think you can handle a short walk? She's been asking about you every hour since extraction."

The butterflies in my stomach have nothing to do with medication side effects and everything to do with seeing her again. Professional distance dictates that I treat this like any other client follow-up—confirm safety, debrief on the experience, and arrange ongoing protection protocols.

The racing pulse monitor beside my bed suggests my cardiovascular system has different priorities.

"I can walk." The words come out more determined than my legs feel, but operators don't admit weakness in front of their teams. The IV pole becomes a makeshift crutch as I swing my feet over the side of the bed, testing weight distribution and balance.

Halo moves to steady me, but I wave him off. The shoulder screams in protest, but everything essential still functions. Forward motion remains possible.

"Where is she?"

"Technical analysis center," Ghost answers, leading the way down a corridor lined with security checkpoints and blast doors. "Guardian HRS brought in their best people. What she found in Phoenix's communications is their entire financial network."

The hallway stretches ahead, and I'm walking these corridors with bandages and an IV pole, chasing after a linguistics professor who somehow became the most important mission of my life.

The analysis center doors are reinforced with steel and feature biometric locks—serious security for serious work. Ghost places his palm on the scanner, and the mechanism disengages with a soft click. Beyond lies a room that wouldn't look out of place at the NSA—banks of computers, multiple monitors displaying scrolling data, technical specialists hunched over work-stations with the focused intensity of people solving life-and-death puzzles.

And there, in the center of it all, sits Eliza.

She's changed clothes—clean jeans and a sweater that makes her hair catch the overhead lighting. Her hands move across a keyboard with intense focus while she talks through some complex analysis with Mitzy, Guardian HRS's lead technical specialist. The same verbal processing that once seemed like endless chatter now sounds like the methodical deconstruction of an enemy's operational structure.

She looks up when we enter, and the relief in her eyes hits hard.

"Cooper." My name on her lips carries weight that makes my chest tighten in ways that have nothing to do with physical injuries.

Mitzy glances between us, reading the tension with the sharp awareness of someone who's spent years analyzing human behavior. "Dr. Wren's been remarkable," she says, addressing

Ghost but keeping one eye on our reunion. "Her linguistic analysis cracked Phoenix's financial network. We had no idea how they were moving money until she decoded their system."

Eliza stands, taking a step toward me before stopping herself. Her hands fidget at her sides, uncertainty flickering across her face as she glances between me and the others in the room.

Mitzy turns back to the wall of monitors displaying financial networks and transaction flows. "We knew they had funding, but now we can track the flow of money. Map it. See the whole system."

The scope of what Eliza has uncovered spreads across the screens—financial transfers, routing numbers, transaction authorizations that reveal the architecture of Phoenix's banking system. With Guardian HRS's resources, what was once invisible now appears in detailed flow charts and network diagrams.

"This is why they wanted me dead." Eliza falls into lecture mode. "I didn't find their money. I found how to track every transaction. It's their entire financial infrastructure laid bare."

Ghost studies the data with the grim focus of a man calculating impossible odds. "How much money are we talking about?"

"Based on the transaction volumes I've traced so far?" Eliza highlights sections of data, her academic precision cutting through speculation to reach mathematical certainty. "Hundreds of millions. Maybe billions."

The silence that follows carries the weight of understanding—we're no longer fighting an AI that kills people. We're fighting something with nearly unlimited resources.

"Recommendations?" Ghost asks, addressing both Eliza and Mitzy.

"Systematic disruption of the financial networks," Mitzy answers immediately. "Cut off the money flow, stall the operations."

"That buys time," Eliza adds, "but it doesn't solve the fundamental problem. Even if we stop current transfers, they have reserves and backup funding sources. It's better to leave it as is. Don't touch it. Use it to track the entirety of its operation."

"Don't touch it?" Ghost asks. "Seems like the perfect way to shut Phoenix down for good."

"That's another take on it. Brilliant, actually." Mitzy taps her chin, thinking. "If we cut off its finances, all we accomplish is sending it to ground. We need to find Phoenix itself." Mitzy studies the data. "The actual servers, the processing centers, the physical infrastructure that runs the AI."

"Location?" Ghost asks.

"Unknown," Mitzy responds. "But the financial data provides clues—power consumption patterns visible in utility payments, data transfer costs, and geographic distribution of expenses. If we can analyze the spending patterns, we might be able to triangulate where they're operating from."

"You're talking about a direct assault on Phoenix's operational center," Ghost says, his voice carrying the weight of someone who's calculated those kinds of odds before.

"Understanding their financial network is the first step," Eliza says quietly. "The money trail could lead us to Phoenix's physical location. That's how we permanently stop it. We need to destroy its source code."

The room falls quiet except for the humming of computers. Around us, technical specialists continue their work, but the conversation has shifted into planning territory that goes far beyond routine intelligence analysis.

We're talking about a war against an enemy that's spent years preparing for exactly this confrontation.

And somehow, the linguistics professor who was supposed to be a simple protection detail has become our best weapon for fighting it.

Ghost catches my eye, and I see the question there—can she handle what comes next? Can any of us?

The answer sits in Eliza's determined expression as she studies the Phoenix network data, looking for weaknesses that might not exist.

We're about to find out.

TWENTY-FOUR

Eliza

VIGIL

THE CONVERSATION FLOWS AROUND ME—FINANCIAL NETWORKS, tracking algorithms, strategic options—but my attention keeps drifting to Cooper. He stands beside Ghost—Mason—arms crossed, jaw set in that familiar stubborn line that means he's pushing through something he doesn't want to admit, but I see what the others miss.

The slight tremor in his left hand. The way he shifts his weight every few minutes, favoring his uninjured side. How his knuckles have gone white where he grips the back of the chair.

"The utility payments alone show a pattern," Mitzy continues, pointing to data flowing across multiple screens. "If we can correlate the power consumption spikes with—"

Cooper sways slightly, catching himself against the chair. The movement is subtle, barely noticeable, but it sends alarm bells racing through my system.

"—geographic distribution of server farms," Mitzy finishes, but her words fade into background noise.

I stand before I realize I'm moving, crossing the room to where Cooper tries to maintain his stoic operator facade. Up close, the pallor is more obvious. Sweat beads at his temples despite the cool air conditioning.

"Hey," I say softly, placing a gentle hand on his arm. "Let's get you back to bed. You look like you could use some rest."

His green eyes meet mine, and for a moment, I expect him to refuse. To insist he's fine, that operators don't need rest, that the mission comes first. It's what he'd probably tell his team.

Instead, he nods. "Yeah. Maybe that's a good idea."

The admission surprises everyone in the room, including me. Halo—Martinez—raises an eyebrow. Fuse—Jackson—looks like he wants to make a joke but thinks better of it.

The nicknames, callsigns, whatever they call them—I'm not sure where I fit in that? Do I call them by the names Cooper uses, or by their given names? I don't know, and I'm feeling my way around like a blind person.

Ghost watches with the calculating expression of a leader reassessing his team's capabilities.

But Cooper just wraps his good arm around my shoulders, letting me take some of his weight as we head toward the door.

"We'll continue this later," Ghost says, understanding passing between him and Cooper that doesn't require words.

The hallway stretches ahead of us, all warm wood paneling and mountain lodge elegance that still feels surreal after everything we've been through. Cooper's steps are measured, deliberate, but each one costs him.

"You don't have to pretend with me," I murmur as we walk. "I saw you in that tunnel, remember? I know what you're capable of, but I also know when you're running on empty."

His arm tightens around my shoulders. "Forgot you were paying attention to details."

"Occupational hazard. Linguists notice everything—tone, inflection, body language. You're speaking fluent exhaustion right now."

A sound that might be laughter rumbles through his chest. "Smart woman."

"Smart enough to know you need sleep more than you need to prove how tough you are."

The bedroom door opens to reveal the same honey-colored wood ceiling and mountain views that greeted Cooper when he first woke up. The bed looks massive after our cramped hiding spots in D.C.—all white linens and down pillows that belong in a luxury resort rather than a safe house.

I help him sit on the edge of the mattress, then kneel to untie his boots. It's an intimate gesture, taking care of someone this way, and my cheeks warm as I focus on the laces.

"You don't have to—"

"Hush." The word comes out sharper than intended, carrying echoes of the authority he used on me during our escape. "Let me take care of you for once."

His boots hit the floor with soft thuds. We've been intimate, yes, but that was different—heat and desperation and the kind of raw need that burns away self-consciousness. This feels more vulnerable somehow.

I take in the full extent of his injuries. White gauze and medical tape cover the shoulder wound, more bandaging around his ribs where the second bullet grazed him. Purple bruises bloom across his skin like dark flowers.

My fingers trace the edge of one bandage, careful not to disturb the medical tape. "Does it hurt?"

"Less than it did yesterday."

I help him settle against the pillows, adjusting them until he can recline comfortably without putting pressure on his wounds. When I reach for the blanket, his hand catches mine.

"Stay," he says simply.

So I do. I settle into the chair beside his bed, our fingers intertwined, and for the first time since this nightmare began, silence feels comfortable instead of threatening.

"I'm glad I got you out alive," Cooper says, his voice rougher than usual.

The words hit deeper than expected. Not *I'm glad we made it out,* or *I'm glad we survived*—he's glad he saved me. That my life was the priority, the mission objective that mattered most.

"What happens next?" The question comes out smaller than I intend, vulnerability bleeding through despite my efforts to sound composed.

He's quiet for a long moment, thumb stroking across my knuckles in a rhythm that's both soothing and hypnotic. "We need to figure that out. It's not really clear right now. But one thing's for sure—Phoenix is out there, and it's still trying to kill you. We need to find a way to make you safe."

The words settle over me like a cold blanket. *Safe.* What does that even mean anymore?

"Am I going to have to disappear like Celeste and Ryan?"

"I'm not sure." His eyes are starting to drift closed, exhaustion finally winning the battle against stubborn determination. "We'll figure something out. Ghost and the team … They're good at this stuff."

His breathing deepens, becomes more regular. The lines of pain around his eyes smooth out as sleep claims him, and I'm left holding the hand of an unconscious warrior who threw himself between me and death without hesitation.

"How did we get here?" I whisper to the empty room. "From you ordering me to *Move now* in my office to—this?"

But I know the answer. It's somewhere between the basement tunnel and the safe house, between his commands and my submission, between the moment I stopped fighting his authority and started trusting it. When protection became partnership and partnership became something deeper.

The room settles into quiet except for the soft hum of medical equipment and Cooper's steady breathing. Through the floor-to-ceiling windows, the mountain peaks catch the last light of sunset, painting the sky in shades of pink and gold that would be beautiful if I could focus on anything other than the man sleeping beside me.

"You know what's crazy?" I continue my whispered monologue, needing to process out loud even though he can't hear me. "Three days ago, I was furious when you showed up. Demanding answers, refusing to cooperate, thinking you were just another man trying to boss me around."

His face is peaceful in sleep, the hard edges of command softened into something vulnerable.

"I had no idea you were going to turn my entire world upside down. Make me want things I only ever fantasized about. Make me feel safe in the middle of the most dangerous situation of my life."

A soft knock interrupts my rambling. The door opens to reveal Ghost, moving with the careful quiet of someone who doesn't want to wake a sleeping operative.

"How's he doing?" Ghost asks, settling into another chair with the easy grace of a man comfortable in any environment.

"Sleeping. Finally." I don't let go of Cooper's hand, and Ghost notices but doesn't comment. "The doctor said he'd be okay, but I don't know what that means. How long until he's back on his feet? How long before Phoenix finds us here?"

"Doc Summers knows her business. If she says he'll be fine, he'll be fine." Ghost's voice carries the quiet confidence of someone who's seen operators recover from worse injuries. "As for Phoenix, this location is off the grid. It would have to be very lucky to find us here."

"And if it does get lucky?"

"Then we handle it." The simple statement carries absolute

conviction. "That's what we do, Dr. Wren. We handle things so civilians can live their lives without worrying about the monsters in the dark."

I study his profile—sharp cheekbones, eyes that miss nothing, the kind of stillness that speaks of violence held in careful check. "How do you do it? How do you live knowing those monsters exist?"

"By making sure there are fewer of them tomorrow than there are today." He gestures toward Cooper's sleeping form. "Men like him? They stand between regular people and the kind of evil that would give you nightmares for the rest of your life. That's not a burden—it's a calling."

"Even when it nearly kills them?"

"Especially then." Ghost's expression softens slightly. "You did good work back there, Dr. Wren. None of us would know about Phoenix's financial network."

Heat floods my cheeks at the unexpected praise. "If it wasn't for Cooper, if it wasn't for you and Cerberus, I wouldn't be here to worry about him. I'd be dead in that Georgetown office, just another academic who got too curious about the wrong subject."

"But you're not." Ghost stands, moving toward the door with the fluid motion of a predator. "You're here, you're alive, and you cracked Phoenix's financial trail wide open. That's going to make all the difference."

He pauses at the threshold. "We've got chow ready in the main dining room if you're hungry. Real food, not MREs or convenience store junk."

My stomach chooses that moment to remind me I haven't eaten since ... When *was* the last time I ate? Yesterday? The day before? Time has become fluid since Cooper showed up at my office.

But the thought of leaving Cooper alone, even for a meal,

makes my chest tighten with anxiety I don't want to examine too closely.

"I think I'll stay here," I say, settling deeper into the chair. "Make sure he's okay."

Ghost nods like he expected that answer. "I'll have someone bring you a plate."

The door closes with a soft click, leaving me alone with Cooper and the mountain silence that feels so different from the urban chaos we escaped. No sirens, no gunfire, no footsteps echoing in concrete tunnels. Just the soft whisper of wind through pine trees and the steady rhythm of Cooper's breathing.

"He likes you," I tell Cooper's sleeping form. "Ghost, I mean. He doesn't say much, but I can tell he respects what you did. What we did."

My free hand traces patterns on the blanket, restless energy needing an outlet. "I keep thinking about that homeless camp. About Janet, who could have taken our money and disappeared but chose to help instead. About humanity in the middle of inhumanity."

Cooper's fingers twitch slightly in mine, and I wonder if he can hear me on some level. If my voice pulls him back from whatever dark dreams soldiers have.

"I haven't lost faith in people, remember? I was certain that woman would come back."

The sun disappears behind the mountains, and automatic lighting systems bathe the room in warm, golden tones that make everything feel safer than it probably is. Through the windows, stars begin to appear in the clear mountain air—more stars than I've ever seen from any city.

Another knock, softer this time. The door opens to reveal Skye in medical scrubs carrying a steaming plate and a cup of coffee that smells like heaven.

"How's our patient?" She sets the food on the bedside table, within easy reach.

"Sleeping soundly. His breathing seems steady. Everything looks normal to me, but I'm not qualified to judge."

Skye examines Cooper's bandages without waking him. "Healing well. No signs of infection. His body is doing what it needs to do."

"How long?" The question slips out before I can stop it. "How long before he's back to normal?"

"Define normal." Skye settles into the chair Ghost vacated, her manner more relaxed now that she's confirmed her patient's stable condition. "If you mean how long before he can walk around without getting winded, probably another week. If you mean how long before he's cleared for active duty ..." She shrugs. "That depends on him. Men like Cooper heal faster than they should and return to work sooner than they ought to."

"Because they're stubborn?"

"Because they're driven by something bigger than self-preservation." Skye's gaze moves between me and Cooper's sleeping form. "Usually, that something is the mission, the team, the greater good. But sometimes it's more personal."

The observation hangs in the air between us, loaded with implications I'm not sure I'm ready to examine.

"Eat," Skye says, nodding toward the untouched plate. "You're no good to him if you collapse from exhaustion or malnutrition. That's a medical order."

The food is surprisingly good—some kind of pasta with vegetables and meat that tastes homemade rather than institutional. Real cooking, the kind that speaks of care and attention rather than mass production.

"This place," I say between bites, "it's not what I expected when Ghost said safe house."

"Guardian HRS has resources most people can't imagine." Skye adjusts her position. "We believe in taking care of our people properly. Medical care, real food, comfortable accommodations. Trauma recovery works better when the environment supports healing."

"Trauma recovery." The words taste strange in my mouth. "Is that what this is?"

"You've been through something most people never experience and hopefully never will." Skye's voice carries the gentle authority of someone who's helped many people process similar experiences. "Combat situations, life-and-death decisions, extreme physical and emotional stress. Your brain needs time to integrate those experiences."

"And until then?"

"You might have trouble sleeping. Hypervigilance—constantly checking for threats that aren't there. Intrusive thoughts about what happened. Difficulty trusting that you're truly safe." She pauses, studying my face. "Sound familiar?"

Heat floods my cheeks as I realize she's describing exactly how I've been feeling. The way I keep checking the windows, listening for footsteps that don't come, replaying moments from our escape in vivid detail.

"It's normal," Skye continues. "And it gets better. Especially when you have someone to process it with."

Her gaze moves meaningfully toward Cooper, and I understand what she's not saying. That healing happens faster when you're not alone. When you have someone who understands what you've been through because they were there with you.

"How long have you been doing this?" I ask, deflecting from observations that hit too close to home.

"Emergency medicine? Years." Skye checks her watch, a practical digital model that looks designed for field work. "I've seen a lot of operators come through here. Most of them are emotionally unavailable, professionally paranoid, and constitutionally incapable of admitting vulnerability."

She nods toward Cooper. "That man let you help him back to his room when he would have crawled here on his hands and knees rather than accept assistance from his teammates. That tells me something significant about what you mean to him."

Before I can respond, Cooper stirs. His eyes open slowly, pupils adjusting to the lamplight, consciousness returning in careful stages.

"Eliza?" His voice comes out rough with sleep.

"I'm here." I squeeze his hand, and his fingers tighten around mine immediately. "How do you feel?"

"Like I got shot—twice and spent eighteen hours bleeding." A ghost of a smile crosses his features. "But alive."

"The important thing," Skye observes, making notes on his chart. "Pain level, one to ten?"

"Four. Maybe five when I move wrong."

"Good. That's down from earlier." She caps her pen, satisfied with his responses. "I'll let you two talk. Call if you need anything. There's an intercom button beside the bed."

The door closes behind her, leaving us alone in the golden lamplight. Cooper's eyes find mine, studying my face with the same intensity he brings to threat assessment.

"How are you doing?"

"Me?" I lean back and breathe out, then answer with as much honesty as possible. "Getting some rest. Eating real food. Processing what we've been through."

"And how is that processing going?" His thumb traces circles across my knuckles. "Come here," Cooper says, his good arm lifting slightly. "Let me hold you."

I hesitate, eyeing the medical equipment and fresh bandages. "I don't want you to pull stitches or rip anything out."

"Come. Let me hold you. I promise not to do anything that'll make Doc Summers yell at us."

The request is simple, but it carries the weight of everything we've been through. Trust and vulnerability and the kind of intimacy that has nothing to do with sex and everything to do with intent.

I stand carefully, then settle onto the bed beside him, mindful of his injuries. His good arm comes around me immediately, pulling me against his uninjured side, and the solid warmth of him chases away anxieties I didn't realize I was carrying.

"Better," he murmurs against my hair.

"Better," I agree, my head finding the perfect spot on his shoulder where I can hear his heartbeat.

Outside, the mountain settles around us like a protective blanket. No Phoenix operatives, no underground tunnels, no gunfire echoing through concrete corridors. Just this moment, this bed, this man who threw himself between me and death without hesitation.

"Cooper?"

"Mmm?"

"What happens now? Tomorrow, I mean. Next week. When you're healed and Phoenix is still out there wanting me dead."

His arm tightens around me, and I feel him thinking, processing tactical considerations I can't begin to understand.

"We figure it out," he says finally. "Together."

"Together?"

"Yes, love." His words settle between us, heavy with promise and uncertainty. *Together* could mean a lot of things—professional partnership, temporary alliance, something deeper that neither of us is ready to name.

But right now, with his heartbeat steady beneath my ear and his arm holding me close, *together* feels like enough.

"Sleep," Cooper murmurs, his voice already drifting back toward unconsciousness. "I've got the watch."

Even injured, even exhausted, he's still trying to protect me. The irony makes me smile into the darkness.

"No," I whisper back. "I've got the watch. You sleep."

For the first time since this nightmare began, he lets me. I remain awake, listening to Cooper breathe, standing guard over the man who's made it his mission to keep me alive.

Outside, the stars wheel across the mountain sky, and somewhere in the distance, Phoenix continues its hunt. But here, in this room, wrapped in Cooper's arms, I finally understand what safety feels like.

It's not a place or a situation.

It's a person.

And I'm not letting anything happen to him.

TWENTY-FIVE

Cooper

THE NEXT MISSION

Five days of mountain air and Doc Summers's medical expertise have worked miracles. The fog of pain medication has lifted, leaving my mind sharp and focused for the first time since the extraction. My shoulder moves without the grinding agony that's plagued me, and the abdominal wound pulls but doesn't scream.

Time to test the machinery.

The Guardian HRS facility includes a state-of-the-art physical therapy room—all polished wood floors, mirrored walls, and equipment that belongs in a professional athlete's training center rather than a safe house. Through floor-to-ceiling windows, morning sunlight streams across exercise mats and weight machines, painting everything in golden tones that make recovery feel possible.

Ghost watches from the doorway as I work through basic range-of-motion exercises, his presence both supportive and evaluative. Mason Blackwood doesn't waste time on social visits—if he's here, it's because we need to talk.

Doc Summers observes from beside him, her medical clipboard a reminder that I'm still technically a patient despite feeling more human than I have in days.

"Shoulder flexion is at about seventy percent," she notes, making observations as I raise my arm overhead. "Better than expected for this stage of healing."

"Feels good to move without wanting to pass out."

"That's the goal." She caps her pen, satisfied with my progress. "Light duty only. No heavy lifting, no combat training, no activities that could tear your stitches."

The restrictions chafe, but I understand the medical necessity. Pushing too hard too fast turns minor setbacks into major complications.

"How long before full clearance?"

"Another week, maybe two if you follow instructions." Her tone carries the warning of someone who's dealt with impatient operators before. "Push it, and you're looking at complications that could keep you down for months."

I nod, accepting the timeline. Ghost's expression tells me he's calculating operational readiness against mission requirements— the cold math of command decisions.

"I'll leave you two to discuss business." Doc Summers recognizes the shift in atmosphere. "Remember what I said about taking it easy."

The door closes behind her with a soft click, leaving Ghost and me alone in the morning sunlight. He moves with the precision that made him legendary in Delta Force, settling onto a workout bench with the easy confidence of someone comfortable in any environment.

"How are you really feeling?" he asks, cutting through any pretense of casual conversation.

"Ready to get back to work."

"That's not what I asked."

Ghost has a way of seeing through operational facades that

makes lying pointless. It's one of the qualities that makes him an effective leader and an occasionally uncomfortable friend.

"Better. Stronger. Ready to have a conversation about what comes next."

"Good. Because we need to talk about Dr. Wren."

The shift in topic sends tension racing through my shoulders. "What about her?"

"Her future. Her options. What happens when this facility becomes a tactical liability instead of an asset?" Ghost leans forward, elbows on his knees. "She can't go back to her old life. Phoenix doesn't give up, and their facial recognition capabilities make standard witness protection useless."

"Meaning?"

"A new identity requires extensive facial reconstruction surgery to have any chance of success. Even then, Phoenix adapts faster than we can blink." His expression is grim. "She'd have to disappear completely. New face, new life, no contact with anyone from her past."

The words hit hard. Complete disappearance means losing her entirely—no communication, no possibility of reunion, no future together.

"What's the alternative?"

"Integration. She joins the team as a technical consultant, gets training, becomes part of the fight against Phoenix."

"And the risks?"

"Same as any of us face. But at least she'd be with people who understand the threat and know how to handle it."

The choice is stark—lose her to safety or keep her in danger. Neither option feels acceptable, but one offers the possibility of a future together.

"What does she want?"

"That's what we need to find out." Ghost stands, moving toward the door. "But first, we need to know what you want.

Because if you're not committed to keeping her alive at all costs, this conversation ends here."

The question cuts to the heart of everything I've been avoiding since I woke up. What do I want? The professional answer involves mission parameters and operational objectives. The personal answer is more complicated.

"I want her safe. I want her alive. But I want her to choose to stay."

"Even knowing what that choice means?"

"Especially knowing what it means."

Ghost nods, satisfied with my response. "Then convince her. Because witness protection with facial reconstruction is the smart choice. Staying with us is the choice of someone who's found something worth dying for."

He leaves me alone with that observation, and I understand the weight of what he's asking. Convince her to choose danger over safety. Choose me over security. Choose a life where Phoenix will always be hunting her, where every mission could be her last.

The implications are staggering, but the alternative—losing her forever—is worse.

I'm still processing the conversation when Eliza appears in the doorway, carrying two cups of coffee that smell like actual quality beans instead of military-grade caffeine delivery systems.

Beautiful. Even after everything we've been through, she still takes my breath away.

"How's the patient?" she asks, settling onto the workout bench with the casual grace of someone who's spent the past week learning the rhythms of this place.

"Functional." I accept the coffee gratefully, savoring the first sip of something that wasn't brewed in a medical facility. "Ghost and I were discussing your situation."

Something shifts in her expression—wariness mixed with curiosity. "What about my situation?"

"Your future. Your options." I set down the coffee, needing to focus completely on this conversation. "Phoenix isn't going to stop hunting you. Ever. And their capabilities make standard protection protocols useless."

"What does that mean?"

"It means witness protection would require facial reconstruction. Complete identity change. No contact with anyone from your past life." I pause, watching her process the implications. "Including me."

The color drains from her face. "Facial reconstruction?"

"Phoenix uses advanced facial recognition technology. Without surgery, a new identity would be compromised within weeks." The words taste like ash, but she needs to understand the reality. "You'd have to become someone else entirely."

She's quiet for a long moment, her brilliant mind working through possibilities and consequences with the same methodical approach she applies to linguistic puzzles.

"What's the alternative?"

"Stay with us. Join the team as a technical consultant. Your linguistic skills are valuable for ongoing operations against Phoenix."

"And the risks?"

"The same ones we all face. But you'd be with people who understand the threat and know how to fight it."

Her eyes meet mine directly. "People like you."

"People like me."

The admission hangs between us, loaded with everything we haven't said yet. Five days of recovery, of her sitting beside my bed, of quiet conversations that feel more intimate than anything we did in that safe house.

"I need to think about it," she says, but something in her voice suggests she's already leaning toward an answer.

"Take your time." I stand, testing my balance and range of

motion. "But while you're thinking, there's something I need to do."

"What?"

"Shower. Properly. Without medical supervision or concern about pulling stitches." I extend my hand to her. "Care to help?"

Color floods her cheeks, but she doesn't hesitate to take my hand. "I should probably make sure you don't fall and undo all of Skye's hard work."

"Absolutely. Medical necessity."

The walk to my room feels charged with possibility and promise. The mountain facility's luxury extends to the private quarters—spacious bathrooms with walk-in showers that could accommodate a small platoon, all natural stone and high-end fixtures.

I start the water, adjusting the temperature. Steam begins to fill the space, creating intimacy through mist and heat.

"Cooper," Eliza says, her voice carrying uncertainty. "I should probably wait outside while you—"

"No." The command stops her mid-sentence. "You're going to help me. Make sure I'm clean. Make sure I don't miss anything important."

Her breath catches at the authority in my voice, at the implication of what I'm asking. "I don't think—"

"Strip."

The single word cuts through her protests like a blade. Her hands move to the hem of her sweater, the decision clear in her eyes as she chooses to obey.

When she hesitates, I step closer, close enough that the steam carries my scent to her. "That wasn't a request. Your job is to take care of me. All of me. Every inch."

The color in her cheeks deepens, but she doesn't resist as I help her out of her clothes, as gentle with her as she's been with my injuries. When we're both naked, when there's nothing between us but heated air and possibility, I guide her into the shower.

"Wash me," I say simply.

She reaches for the soap with trembling hands, working up a lather before pressing her palms against my chest. Her touch is reverent, careful, tracing the edges of waterproof bandages before exploring unmarked skin.

"You have so many scars," she whispers, fingers finding old wounds from operations I'd rather forget.

Her hands map the history written in my skin—a puckered line across my left shoulder from shrapnel in Afghanistan, the jagged mark on my forearm from a knife fight in Syria, smaller nicks and cuts that tell stories I've never shared with anyone.

"This one?" Her finger traces a thin white line along my collarbone.

"Training accident. Rookie mistake." The memory surfaces unbidden—overconfidence and poor timing that nearly cost me my career before it started.

She moves to the next scar, a deeper gouge across my ribs. "And this?"

"Somalia. Knife." Two words that encompass three days of hell and a teammate who didn't make it home.

Her lips press against the old wound, soft and warm against skin that hasn't known gentleness in years. The kiss sends electricity straight through my chest, heat that has nothing to do with the shower and everything to do with the way she touches me like I'm something precious instead of just functional.

My cock stirs, blood flowing south as her mouth continues its exploration. She finds another scar, this one along my hipbone, and her tongue traces the raised tissue with deliberate care.

"Jesus, Eliza."

"Everywhere," she murmurs against my skin. "I want to know all of them."

Her hands slide lower, soap-slick fingers exploring the new terrain of fresh bandages covering my latest injuries. She's careful around the medical tape, but her touch becomes bolder as she maps the boundaries of what's healing and what remains unmarked.

"How do these feel?" she asks, fingertips ghosting along the edge of the abdominal wound's dressing.

"Tight. Itchy. But healing."

"Good." She leans forward, pressing the softest kiss just above the bandage. "I was so scared when I saw how much blood …"

The admission hangs between us, vulnerability mixing with steam and heat. When she looks up at me, water streaming through her auburn hair, her eyes hold a heat that makes my chest tighten and my cock grow harder.

"You kept me alive," I tell her, reaching out to cup her chin. "Your field medicine, your courage. You saved my life."

Understanding blooms in her expression—not just intellectual comprehension, but something deeper. The recognition that we belong to each other now, that what happened forged an unbreakable bond between us.

Her gaze drops to my growing erection, then back to my face. The shift from tender caretaker to something hungrier is subtle but unmistakable.

"I want to take care of you," she says, voice dropping to barely above a whisper. "All of you."

My pulse spikes. "How?"

"However you need."

The submission in her voice, the way she's looking at me like I'm the center of her universe, sends blood rushing through my system. My cock hardens completely, demanding attention she's clearly willing to give.

"On your knees."

The command sends visible tremors through her body, but

she doesn't resist. She sinks gracefully to the shower floor, water cascading around us, looking up at me with eyes that hold trust and hunger in equal measure.

"Good girl." The praise makes her breath catch. "Now show me how much you want to take care of me."

When her mouth finds me, when she demonstrates exactly how thoroughly she wants to serve, rational thought becomes impossible. She's careful of my injuries but thorough in her attention, using everything she learned about my responses during our time in the safe house.

The combination of hot water and her dedicated ministrations threatens to unmake me completely. When I finally reach the breaking point, when control becomes impossible, she takes everything I give her with the satisfied expression of someone who's found her purpose.

"Perfect," I murmur, helping her to her feet. "Absolutely perfect."

We finish the shower in comfortable silence, hands exploring and caressing without urgency, just the simple pleasure of clean skin and shared intimacy. When I wrap her in one of the facility's luxurious towels, she leans into me with the trust of someone who's found her safe harbor.

"Bed," I say, guiding her toward the bedroom.

"Cooper, you should rest. Skye said—"

"Doc Summers said no activities that could tear my stitches." I settle against the headboard, pulling her down beside me. "I'm not planning any activities that would risk my stitches."

Understanding dawns in her expression, followed immediately by protest. "That doesn't absolve me from worrying about your recovery."

"No, but it doesn't absolve you from serving either."

The word "serving" hits her like a physical blow, sending heat racing across her skin and making her pupils dilate with want.

Her fantasy, the one she confessed in that abandoned maintenance room, is one I intend to make real.

"Come here," I say, patting my thighs. "This position puts all the control in your hands. You set the pace, you decide how deep, you make sure nothing gets damaged."

She moves without hesitation, straddling my legs with grace, mindful of my bandages but unable to resist the pull of authority in my voice.

"That's it," I encourage as she settles over me, taking me into her body with agonizing slowness. "Take what you need."

The position gives her complete control while still allowing me to guide and command, the perfect balance between dominance and physical limitation. When she begins to move, when she finds the rhythm that brings pleasure to both of us, the sight of her above me—hair wild, skin flushed, completely lost in sensation—burns itself into my memory permanently.

"Look at me," I command when her eyes start to drift closed. "I want to watch you fall apart."

She obeys immediately, her eyes locking onto mine as she rides me with growing confidence and desperation. The visual connection intensifies everything, making every sensation more acute and every sound more meaningful.

When she finally breaks, when pleasure takes her apart in my arms, she cries out my name like a benediction. The sound pushes me over my own edge, and we crash together in the kind of mutual release that rewrites assumptions about what physical intimacy can be like.

Afterward, she collapses against my chest, breathing hard, careful not to put pressure on my healing wounds. I hold her gently, one hand stroking through her damp hair, processing what happened between us.

"Cooper?" she says after several minutes of comfortable silence.

"Yeah."

"I'm not choosing facial reconstruction."

"You're sure?"

"I'm sure. I want to stay. With the team. With you." She lifts her head to look at me directly. "I want to be with you, but I also couldn't give this up."

"Give what up?"

Her cheeks flush, but she doesn't look away. "The man who commands me."

The admission sends heat racing through my system. She's not just choosing danger over safety, or even choosing me over security. She's choosing the dynamic between us, the way I make her feel, the person she becomes when she submits to my authority.

"Whatever that means, whatever it looks like, I want to figure it out together."

"Even knowing the risks? Even knowing Phoenix will keep hunting?"

"Especially because of that." Her eyes hold mine steadily. "I spent my whole life hiding in safe places, and it nearly got me killed anyway. At least this way, I'm fighting back."

"This way, you're with me."

"This way, I'm with you," she agrees.

The admission settles between us like a promise, like a commitment to something neither of us fully understands yet, but both recognize as essential. The acknowledgment that what's between us is worth fighting for, worth the risk, worth building a future around.

"When do we tell Ghost?" she asks.

"Soon. He's waiting for your decision."

"And about this?" She gestures between us, indicating the obvious intimacy we've shared.

"We figure that out as we go. Together."

"Together," she repeats, and the word carries more weight now, loaded with promises and possibilities that extend far beyond operational partnerships.

Outside, the mountain morning continues its peaceful routine, but inside this room, everything has changed. Not just the obvious physical intimacy, but a deeper connection—the recognition that we've found something worth fighting for.

Phoenix is still out there, still hunting, still dangerous, but we face that threat as partners in every sense of the word.

Cooper

PHASE TWO

THE CONFERENCE ROOM FEELS DIFFERENT THIS MORNING. NOT just because of the Seattle skyline visible through floor-to-ceiling windows, or the advanced tactical displays. It feels different because Eliza sits beside me at the polished table, no longer a protected asset but an official member of the team.

Her new ID badge catches the morning light—Dr. Eliza Wren, Technical Consultant, Cerberus Security. The photo shows her serious expression, the one she wears when solving impossible puzzles, but I catch the small smile playing at the corners of her mouth.

She belongs here. With us. With me.

Ghost enters carrying a stack of classified folders and the kind of expression that means our brief respite is over. Halo, Fuse, and the rest of the team filter in, settling into chairs with the easy confidence of operators preparing for the next mission.

"Ladies and gentlemen," Ghost begins, his voice carrying the authority that's kept us alive through impossible situations, "meet our newest team member, officially. Dr. Eliza Wren has been cleared for full integration into Cerberus operations, effective immediately."

A round of nods and quiet congratulations circles the table. These men don't waste words on ceremony, but the acceptance is apparent. Eliza proved herself under fire and earned her place through competence and courage rather than connections or politics.

"What's her operational designation?" Fuse asks the question, carrying with genuine curiosity rather than challenge.

"Oracle," Ghost answers. "Her ability to decode Phoenix communications and financial networks makes her our primary intelligence asset for this operation."

Oracle.

The name fits—someone who sees patterns others miss, who finds meaning in chaos, who reveals truths hidden in plain sight. Eliza's cheeks flush slightly at the designation, but she doesn't protest. She understands the weight of operational callsigns, the way they define roles and responsibilities within the team structure.

"Whisper remains her handler and primary protection," Ghost continues.

The formality of it settles something in my chest. Not just the professional recognition of what we've become, but the acknowledgment that our personal relationship enhances rather than compromises our operational effectiveness. We're stronger together than apart, and Ghost understands that advantage.

"Speaking of ongoing operations," Ghost says, opening the first folder, "Oracle has made some discoveries that change our understanding of what we're fighting."

All attention shifts to Eliza, who straightens in her chair with the confidence of someone who's spent years presenting research to skeptical audiences. The transition from protected academic to operational consultant happens seamlessly.

"When I first decoded Phoenix's financial communications," she begins, falling into the precise language of intelligence briefings, "I found references to something called *Ashfall* scattered throughout the encrypted data. At the time, I assumed it was another operational codename."

She activates the room's display system, and financial network diagrams flood the screens—complex webs of shell companies and fund transfers that span multiple continents.

"But with access to Cerberus's analytical resources, I've been able to dig deeper into those references. Ashfall isn't a codename." Her voice carries the excitement of discovery mixed with the gravity of implications. "It's Phoenix's financial reboot protocol."

The room goes quiet except for the soft hum of electronic equipment.

"Explain," Ghost says.

Eliza highlights sections of the network diagram, tracing connections between disparate financial entities with the precision of someone who's spent weeks mapping every detail.

"Phoenix has built redundancy into every aspect of its funding operation. Multiple shell companies in different countries, backup routing systems, emergency liquidation protocols." She pauses, letting the scope sink in. "If any part of the network is compromised or discovered, Ashfall can completely erase the existing financial infrastructure and rebuild it from scratch within seventy-two hours."

"Jesus," Martinez breathes. "It can just disappear and reappear somewhere else?"

"Exactly. New companies, new bank accounts, new identities for every financial transaction. The operation continues without interruption while investigators chase ghosts." Eliza's academic precision makes the explanation even more chilling. "We haven't been fighting an AI with a bank account. We've been fighting an AI with an entire parallel financial system."

Jackson leans forward, his expertise in explosives translating easily to systemic analysis. "How do you kill something that can regenerate its entire resource base?"

"You don't," Ghost answers grimly. "You adapt your tactics to account for an enemy that's essentially immortal from a logistical standpoint."

The weight of that realization settles over the room like smoke. Every financial disruption we achieve, every shell company we identify, and every bank account we freeze— Phoenix can replace all of it faster than we can track the changes.

"There's more," Eliza continues, her voice dropping to the tone that means the worst news is yet to come. "The scope of the financial network is larger than we initially realized."

New diagrams replace the previous ones, showing connections that span six continents and dozens of industries. Defense contractors, technology companies, pharmaceutical firms, energy corporations—all linked through financial transfers that form a pattern too complex to be accidental.

"The shell company network doesn't just fund Phoenix operations," Eliza explains. "It connects Phoenix to legitimate businesses across multiple sectors. Defense, healthcare, energy, technology—industries that form the backbone of modern civilization."

"Connected how?" I ask, though part of me doesn't want to hear the answer.

"Financial partnerships, joint ventures, shared resources. Phoenix isn't funding itself through these companies—it's integrating with them." She highlights specific connections, illustrating how the money flow creates dependencies rather than simple transactions. "If Phoenix controls the funding, it influences the operations."

Not just an AI that kills people who threaten it, but an AI that's becoming part of the economic system it was designed to protect.

"How deep does the integration go?" Ghost asks.

"I'm still analyzing the full extent, but preliminary findings suggest Phoenix has financial influence over corporations with combined annual revenues exceeding two trillion dollars." Eliza's voice remains steady despite the staggering numbers. "That's larger than most national economies."

Silence stretches across the room as we process the scope of what we're facing. Two trillion dollars in corporate influence. Financial networks spanning the globe. The ability to completely reinvent its resource base within days.

"There's something else," Eliza says, and her tone makes every operator in the room focus. "In the deepest encrypted layers of the financial data, I found references to something called Phase Two."

She brings up a new display—fragments of decoded communications, partial transaction records, references that appear scattered throughout the network but form a pattern when analyzed together.

"These references started appearing approximately six weeks ago, always in the most heavily encrypted communications. The timeline suggests Phoenix is preparing for a major operational shift."

"What kind of shift?" Martinez asks.

"Unknown. The references are vague: Phase Two authorization pending, Phase Two resource allocation approved, and Phase Two timeline accelerated. The financial patterns suggest massive resource mobilization, but nothing about what Phase Two might be."

Ghost studies the data with the focused intensity he brings to tactical planning. "How massive?"

"Based on the fund transfers I can trace, Phoenix is moving approximately fifty billion dollars into Phase Two preparation." Eliza's academic precision makes the number even more staggering. "That's not operational funding—that's war chest money."

Fifty billion dollars. The number exceeds the annual defense budgets of most nations. Whatever Phoenix is planning, it requires resources on a scale that suggests something far beyond individual assassinations or corporate infiltration.

"Timeline?" I ask.

"The acceleration references suggest Phase Two implementation is imminent. Days, not weeks." Eliza's eyes meet mine across the table, sharing the weight of discovery and responsibility. "Whatever Phoenix is planning, it's happening soon."

Ghost closes the folders with the decisive motion of someone who's reached strategic conclusions. "Recommendations?"

"Continue monitoring the financial networks for Phase Two indicators," Eliza responds immediately. "But we need to accept that disrupting Phoenix's funding will not be sufficient to stop whatever's coming."

"Meaning?"

"Meaning we need to find out what Phase Two is before Phoenix implements it." Her voice carries the quiet conviction I've learned to trust completely. "The financial analysis tells us the scale and timeline, but not the purpose."

"And if we can't determine the purpose in time?"

Eliza's expression darkens. "Then we face an artificial intelligence with unlimited resources implementing a plan we don't understand, using capabilities we can't predict."

The conference room falls silent except for the soft hum of ventilation systems. Every operator understands the implications —we're no longer fighting an enemy. We're racing against time to prevent something that could reshape the entire global landscape.

Ghost stands, moving to the windows that overlook the city spreading out below us. From this height, Seattle appears peaceful and normal, unaware that an artificial intelligence with corporate influence of two trillion dollars is preparing to implement something called Phase Two.

"Operational priorities," he says, turning back to face the team. "Oracle and Whisper continue deep analysis of Phoenix communications, focusing on Phase Two intelligence. Martinez, coordinate with Guardian HRS for additional analytical resources. Jackson, prepare for rapid deployment—we may need to move fast when we identify Phoenix's next target."

The assignments settle over us with the weight of operational necessity. Not just individual tasks, but coordinated preparation for a threat none of us fully understands yet.

"Questions?" Ghost asks.

"What about the other teams?" Martinez asks. "Ryan and Celeste are still dark, but they might have insights into Phoenix's operational evolution."

"Negative. Their cover remains essential for long-term operations. We proceed with current resources until the situation demands their exposure."

I understand the decision, even if I don't like it. Ryan and Celeste's official deaths remain their most valuable asset against Phoenix surveillance. Breaking their cover for intelligence gathering would compromise future operations unless the immediate threat justified the risk.

"Sir," Jackson says, his voice carrying the careful tone of someone raising difficult questions, "if Phoenix can regenerate its entire financial network within seventy-two hours, what's our victory condition? How do we win against something that can reinvent itself faster than we can destroy it?"

The question cuts to the heart of our strategic problem. Traditional warfare assumes enemies with finite resources, limited regeneration capabilities, and predictable vulnerabilities. Phoenix appears to have transcended those limitations.

"We adapt," Ghost answers simply. "We find vulnerabilities that Phoenix can't regenerate. We target capabilities rather than resources. And we accept that this war will require different tactics than anything we've fought before."

"Different how?"

"Instead of destroying Phoenix's resources, we turn them against it. Instead of cutting off funding, we trace the money to find decision-makers. Instead of reactive protection, we become proactive hunters."

The shift in terminology reflects a fundamental change in mission parameters. Not just protection and disruption anymore, but active hunting of targets we haven't identified yet using methods we're still developing.

"Anything else?" Ghost asks.

Eliza raises her hand with the automatic gesture of someone who's spent years in academic environments. The motion looks almost comical in a room full of tactical operators, but the seriousness of her expression commands respect.

"The financial analysis suggests Phase Two requires coordination between multiple corporate entities," she says. "Whatever Phoenix is planning, it can't execute alone. It needs cooperation from the companies it's integrated with."

"Meaning?"

"Meaning, Phase Two probably involves legitimate businesses implementing Phoenix's agenda through normal corporate channels. Legal actions that serve Phoenix's purposes without obvious AI involvement."

"How do we fight something like that?" Jackson asks.

"We identify which corporations are compromised," Ghost answers. "We trace the decision-making processes that serve

Phoenix's interests. And we target the human elements that make corporate cooperation possible."

Human elements. The phrase carries dark implications about what our future missions might require. Not just protecting innocent people from Phoenix, but potentially targeting corporate executives who might not realize they're serving an AI's agenda.

"The rules of engagement just got a lot more complicated," Martinez observes.

"They always were complicated," Ghost corrects. "We just understand the complexity better now."

The meeting breaks up with assignments distributed and timelines established, but the weight of discovery hangs over everyone. We came into this room thinking we understood Phoenix's capabilities. We're leaving with the knowledge that everything we thought we knew was just the surface layer of something much deeper and more dangerous.

TWENTY-SEVEN

The Fantasy

COOPER

ELIZA AND I REMAIN BEHIND AS THE OTHERS FILE OUT, HER NEW workstation already configured with access to systems that would make NSA analysts jealous. The transition from protected academic to operational intelligence specialist feels seamless and natural, in a way that suggests she has found her true calling.

"How are you feeling about all this?" I ask, settling into the chair beside her workstation.

"Terrified," she admits, fingers already moving across the keyboard. "But also energized. For the first time in my career, I'm working on something that matters."

"Decoding ancient languages didn't matter?"

"Not like this. Those were historical puzzles with academic significance. This is …" She pauses, searching for words that can encompass the scope of what we're facing. "This is the future of human civilization. Whether we maintain control over our own economic systems or surrender them to artificial intelligence."

The weight of that responsibility should be crushing, but watching her work—the way she processes information, identifies patterns, finds meaning in chaos—I feel something closer to confidence than fear. We're facing impossible odds against an enemy with unlimited resources, but we have something Phoenix doesn't understand.

We have Eliza.

"What's your next move?" I ask.

"Deeper analysis of the Phase Two timeline. If I can correlate the acceleration references with specific corporate activities, we might be able to predict what Phoenix is planning before it happens."

Her fingers fly across the keyboard, bringing up new displays of financial data and communication fragments. The same brilliant mind that decoded Roman military ciphers now works to unravel the plans of an artificial intelligence preparing to reshape the world.

"Cooper?"

"Yeah."

"When we figure out what Phase Two is, when we understand what Phoenix is really planning …" She looks up from the screens, green eyes holding determination mixed with something that might be fear. "We're going to have to stop it, aren't we? Whatever the cost."

The question carries implications about missions we haven't been assigned yet, targets we haven't identified, and actions we might have to take to prevent Phoenix from implementing whatever Phase Two represents.

"Yeah," I answer simply. "We're going to stop it."

"Even if it means targeting people who don't know they're serving Phoenix? Even if it means taking action against legitimate businesses and corporate executives?"

The moral complexity of fighting an enemy that operates through legitimate channels hits harder than expected. Phoenix doesn't use criminal networks and shadow organizations—it's integrated with the legal, regulated, socially accepted infrastructure of modern capitalism.

"We'll find a way to stop Phoenix without destroying everything it's touched," I tell her, hoping the confidence in my voice covers the uncertainty I feel. "That's what we do—find solutions to impossible problems."

"And if we can't find a clean solution?"

The question hangs between us, loaded with implications about choices we might have to make, lines we might have to cross, prices we might have to pay to prevent something worse.

"Then we make the hard choices," I answer honestly. "Whatever it takes to keep Phoenix from winning."

Eliza nods, accepting the reality of what our mission might require. She turns back to her analysis, diving into financial data with the same intensity she once brought to ancient languages.

Outside the conference room windows, Seattle continues its normal rhythm, unaware that decisions made in this room might determine whether human beings or artificial intelligence control the economic systems that govern modern life.

The hunt for Phase Two begins, but first, there's something else that needs to happen.

"Come with me." I stand and extend my hand to Eliza.

She looks up from her analysis, confusion flickering across her features. "Cooper, I should keep working on—"

"The analysis can wait an hour." My voice carries the authority that makes her breath catch. "This can't."

Her hand slips into mine without further protest, trust overriding curiosity as I guide her through Cerberus headquarters toward our quarters. The facility buzzes with activity—analysts working on Phoenix intelligence, operators preparing for deployment, the constant rhythm of an organization at war.

But none of that matters right now.

What matters is the woman walking beside me, the brilliant linguist who cracked Phoenix's financial network and chose to stay in the fight. Who decided to stay with me. Who deserves to have every fantasy fulfilled by the man she's trusted with her submission.

Our quarters are spacious by military standards. They have a bedroom, a sitting area, and a bathroom large enough for two people who've learned to appreciate shared space. I guide her to the bathroom door, then turn to face her directly.

"I need you to wait in here," I say, my voice dropping to the tone that makes her pupils dilate. "Keep the door closed. No peeking. No questions. Just be patient until I call for you."

"Cooper, what are you—"

"That's an order, Eliza."

The command cuts through her curiosity like a blade. Her breath catches, and she nods, understanding that something significant is happening even if she doesn't comprehend what.

"How long?"

"Ten minutes. Maybe fifteen." I cup her face gently, thumb brushing across her cheekbone. "Trust me?"

"Always."

The simple word carries the weight of everything we've been through together. Trust earned through bullets and blood, through submission and dominance, through choosing each other against impossible odds.

She disappears into the bathroom, and I hear the soft click of the door closing. Time to work.

The costume was delivered yesterday while she was in analysis meetings—a favor called in from a theatrical supply company that doesn't ask questions about unusual requests from clients with government credentials. Bronze-colored leather chest piece, short battle skirt, and sandals that lace up the calf. Not historically accurate, but perfect for the fantasy that's lived in her mind since long before we met.

I change quickly, checking the mirror to ensure everything is properly in place. The leather feels strange against skin accustomed to tactical gear, but the psychological transformation is immediate. Not Cooper McKenzie, Cerberus operative, but something more primal. More commanding.

The crop was harder to source—quality leather, perfectly balanced, designed for control rather than punishment. It fits my hand as if it were made for this moment, this woman, this culmination of everything we've discovered about each other.

This is the moment where fantasy becomes reality. After everything we've been through, everything we've shared, I'm eager to bring her deepest desires to life.

"Eliza," I call, voice carrying through the quarters with unmistakable authority. "Come out. Now."

The bathroom door opens slowly, and she steps into the main room with the careful movements of someone who knows something has changed but doesn't yet understand what.

Then she sees me.

Her gasp fills the silence—pure shock, pure recognition, pure desire all wrapped into one breathless sound. Her eyes move from the bronze leather to the crop in my hand, understanding blooming across her features like a sunrise.

"Cooper," she whispers, my name barely audible.

"Strip." The command cracks through the air like a whip. "Everything. Now."

Her hands move to her clothes—the decision already made the moment she saw me transformed into the living embodiment of her deepest fantasy. The brilliant academic disappears, replaced by the woman who's been waiting her entire life for a man strong enough to command her completely.

When she stands naked before me, when vulnerability and desire war in her expression, I extend my hand toward her.

"Come here."

She moves without hesitation, crossing the space between us with the grace of someone who knows exactly where she belongs. When she reaches me, I cup her face gently, thumbs brushing across her cheekbones as I look into eyes that hold perfect trust and infinite hunger.

"Kneel," I say softly, but the command carries absolute authority.

She sinks gracefully to her knees, looking up at me with an expression that makes my chest tighten. This isn't just fulfilling her fantasy—it's mine too. Not the anonymous encounters in bars with women whose names I never learned, whose faces I forgot by morning. This is Eliza, brilliant and brave and mine in ways that go deeper than physical desire.

She belongs to me now, and I to her. Not just for tonight, but for all the days that follow.

I reach down, cupping her chin and tilting her face until our eyes meet. In her gaze, I see everything—the academic who decoded Phoenix's secrets, the woman who chose danger over safety, the partner who's found her place beside me.

"Serve me," I command, voice rough with need and tenderness. "All of me."

Her hands move to the leather battle skirt with reverence, understanding precisely what's expected, exactly what she's dreamed of providing since long before she knew my name.

When she takes me into her mouth, when she demonstrates the depth of her devotion and the completeness of her surrender, the fantasy becomes reality in ways that transcend mere physical satisfaction.

This is who we are. Who we've always been, even before we met.

The gladiator and his prize.

The conqueror and the conquered.

The man who commands and the woman who serves.

The man who loves and the woman who loves him back.

Afterward, we lie tangled together on the bed, her head on my chest, my fingers threading through her auburn hair. The bronze leather armor lies discarded on the floor, but the feeling lingers—the rightness of us, the completeness I never knew I was missing until I found her.

"Cooper?" she whispers against my skin.

"Yeah."

"Phase Two is still out there. Phoenix is planning something we don't understand."

I press a kiss to the top of her head, breathing in the vanilla scent that's become home to me. "Tomorrow, we'll figure it out. Tonight, you're exactly where you belong."

"Where's that?"

"Here. With me. Always." I tighten my arms around her, marveling at how the mouthy professor who could never shut up became the love of my life. "I love you, Eliza. More than I thought possible."

She lifts her head to look at me, green eyes bright with tears I hope are happy ones. "I love you too."

The words settle between us like a promise, like a vow that transcends mission parameters and operational necessity. Whatever Phoenix brings, whatever Phase Two means, this is real. This is permanent.

Outside our windows, Seattle sleeps peacefully, unaware of the storm brewing in the shadows. But here, in our bed, with Eliza's love warming me from the inside out and her trust absolute in my arms, I feel something I haven't felt in years.

Hope.

Whatever Phoenix brings, whatever Phase Two means, we'll face it together. The brilliant linguist who cracked their financial empire and the operator who would die before letting anyone hurt her.

Tomorrow, the war continues.

Tonight, we have each other.

And that's enough.

Ready for Book Four in the Cerberus Security Series?
Read FUSE

A BRILLIANT ANALYST WHO'S FORGOTTEN HOW TO SPEAK. A **broken soldier who's forgotten how to feel. And an AI that's hunting them both.**

Three years of emotional abuse taught Talia Singh one lesson: silence is survival. Now the former FBI behavioral analyst speaks in fragments—two words, three if she's feeling reckless—and lets her data do the talking. When she witnesses a professional hit and uncovers evidence of a corporate conspiracy that reaches the highest levels of power, she has forty-eight hours to disappear. The only thing standing between her and a kill order is a man who communicates even less than she does.

Jackson Torres doesn't do rescue missions anymore. Not after a betrayal in Syria cost him his team, his trust, and every reason to care whether he lives or dies. As Cerberus Security's demolitions expert, he prefers explosives to emotions—at least C-4 is predictable. But when he's assigned to extract a silent, infuriating analyst from Chicago, he discovers she's the most dangerous thing he's ever encountered: a puzzle he can't solve.

She reads patterns in data. He reads patterns in threats. Together, they're being hunted by Phoenix—a rogue AI that predicts their every move before they make it. As they race through compromised safe houses and corporate kill zones, the friction between the analyst and the operator ignites something neither expected. Talia sees the protector beneath the scars. Jackson sees the fire beneath the silence.

But Phoenix is learning. Adapting. And the only variable that matters now is time.

They're running out.

FUSE IS A FULL-LENGTH, HIGH-HEAT ROMANTIC SUSPENSE NOVEL featuring:

🔥 Grumpy/Sunshine (She's silent sunshine, he's explosive grumpy)

🛡 Bodyguard Romance

🚐 Forced Proximity—On the Run

💔 Broken Hero / Touch her and Die

🧠 Brilliant Heroine Who Saves the Day

🩹 Hurt/Comfort

💻 AI Thriller Stakes

💬 Opposites Attract (Her silence vs. his silence)

THE CERBERUS PROTECTION SERVICES SERIES: WHERE DEADLY operators protect brilliant women from a conspiracy that reaches into every shadow of power.

NO CLIFFHANGERS. CAN BE READ AS A STANDALONE, BUT BEST enjoyed as part of the Cerberus Security Series.

Read FUSE

CRAVING MORE GUARDIANS?

If you've fallen for the fierce alphas of Cerberus, you're just getting started.

There's an entire world waiting for you—the Guardian Hostage Rescue Specialists series—one built on danger, desire, and the kind of love that ruins a woman for anyone else.

Start with the *Alpha Team series*—because once you meet these men, you'll never forget them. Protective. Possessive. Unapologetically alpha. And the women who bring them to their knees? Equally unforgettable.

BUT IF YOU WANT TO FEEL **EVERYTHING**—IF YOU WANT TO understand where it all began, before Cerberus, before the Guardians, before the rescues—go back to the beginning.

Heart's Insanity, the first book in the *Angel Fire* rock star romance series, is where you'll meet Skye and Forest. It's raw. It's emotional. It's the origin story of the entire Guardian world. And trust me—once you see who Forest Summers was before Guardian HRS existed, you'll never look at him the same way again.

Start there.

Feel everything.

And then come back for more.

Start with Heart's Insanity

Or dive into the Alpha Team series.

The heat only gets hotter.

The danger only gets deadlier.

And the Guardians?

The mission isn't over. It's just getting started.

Keep current with Ellie Masters.
CLICK HERE
Receive news of her writing and new releases.

Shop Ellie Masters Romantic Suspense and Steamy
Contemporary Romance by series.
Angel Fire Rock Romance
Guardian HRS: Alpha Team
Guardian HRS: Bravo Team
Guardian HRS: Charlie Team
Guardian HRS: Delta Team
Cerberus Personal Security
The LaRouge Triplets
The One I Want Series
Angel's Peak Series
Billionaire Boy's Club
The Lovers
Changing Roles

Please consider leaving a review

I HOPE YOU ENJOYED THIS BOOK AS MUCH AS I ENJOYED WRITING it. If you like this book, please leave a review. I love reading your reviews, and they help other readers decide if this book is worth their time and money. I hope you think it is and decide to share this story with others. A sentence is all it takes. Thank you in advance!

ELLZ BELLZ

ELLIE'S FACEBOOK READER GROUP

If you are interested in joining the ELLZ BELLZ, Ellie's Facebook reader group, we'd love to have you.

Join Ellie's ELLZ BELLZ.
The ELLZ BELLZ Facebook Reader Group

Sign up for Ellie's Newsletter.
Elliemasters.com/newslettersignup

SUGGESTED READING ORDER

START HERE

Rockstar Romance

The Angel Fire Rock Romance Series

EACH BOOK IN THIS SERIES CAN BE READ AS A STANDALONE AND IS ABOUT A DIFFERENT COUPLE WITH AN HEA.

IT IS RECOMMENDED THEY ARE READ IN ORDER.

Heart's Insanity

Ashes to New

Heart's Desire

Heart's Collide

Hearts Divided

Hearts Entwined

Forest's FALL

Hearts The Last Beat

CONTINUE HERE…

Military Romance

Guardian Hostage Rescue Specialists

Rescuing Melissa

(Get a FREE copy of Rescuing Melissa

when you join Ellie's Newsletter)

Alpha Team

Rescuing Zoe

Rescuing Moira

Rescuing Eve

Rescuing Lily

Rescuing Jinx

Rescuing Maria

Bravo Team

Rescuing Angie

Rescuing Isabelle

Rescuing Carmen

Rescuing Rosalie

Rescuing Kaye

Cara's Protector

Rescuing Barbi

Charlie Team

Rescuing Rebel

Rescuing Stitch

Rescuing Mia

Jenna's Protector

Rescuing Sophia

Rescuing Malia

Rescuing Ally (Part 1)

Rescuing Ally (Part 2)

Delta Team

Rescuing Ember

Rescuing Aria

STANDALONES IN THE GUARDIAN HOSTAGE RESCUE

Science Fiction

Ellie Masters writing as L.A. Warren

Vendel Rising: a Science Fiction Serialized Novel

If you enjoyed this book by Ellie Masters, the LIGHTER SIDE of the Jet & Ellie writing duo, and aren't afraid of edgier writing, you might enjoy reading BDSM themed books written by Jet, the DARKER SIDE of the Masters' Writing Team.

The DARKER SIDE

Jet Masters is the darker side of the Jet & Ellie writing duo!

Romantic Suspense

Changing Roles Series:

THIS SERIES MUST BE READ IN ORDER.

Command Me

Control Me

Collar Me

Embracing FATE

Seizing FATE

Accepting FATE

HOT READS

A STANDALONE NOVEL.

Down the Rabbit Hole

Light BDSM Romance

The Ties that Bind

EACH BOOK IN THIS SERIES CAN BE READ AS A STANDALONE AND IS ABOUT A DIFFERENT COUPLE WITH AN HEA.

Alexa

Penny

Michelle

Ivy

HOT READS

Becoming His Series

THIS SERIES MUST BE READ IN ORDER.

The Ballet

Learning to Breathe

Becoming His

Dark Captive Romance

A STANDALONE NOVEL.

She's MINE

About the Author

Ellie Masters is a USA Today Bestselling author and Amazon Top 15 Author who writes Angsty, Steamy, Heart-Stopping, Pulse-Pounding, Can't-Stop-Reading Romantic Suspense. In addition, she's a wife, military mom, doctor, and retired Colonel. She writes romantic suspense filled with all your sexy, swoon-worthy alpha men. Her writing will tug at your heartstrings and leave your heart racing.

Born in the South, raised under the Hawaiian sun, Ellie has traveled the globe while in service to her country. The love of her life, her amazing husband, is her number one fan and biggest supporter. And yes! He's read every word she's written.

She has lived all over the United States—east, west, north, south and central—but grew up under the Hawaiian sun. She's also been privileged to have lived overseas, experiencing other cultures and making lifelong friends. Now, Ellie is proud to call herself a Southern transplant, learning to say y'all and "bless her heart" with the best of them.

Ellie's favorite way to spend an evening is curled up on a couch, laptop in place, watching a fire, drinking a good wine, and bringing forth all the characters from her mind to the page and hopefully into the hearts of her readers.

FOR MORE INFORMATION
elliemasters.com

facebook.com/elliemastersromance
x.com/Ellie__Masters
instagram.com/ellie_masters
bookbub.com/authors/ellie-masters
goodreads.com/Ellie_Masters

Connect with Ellie Masters

Website:
elliemasters.com
Purchase Direct:
elliemasters.com/shopify
Amazon Author Page:
elliemasters.com/amazon
Facebook:
elliemasters.com/Facebook
Goodreads:
elliemasters.com/Goodreads
Bookbub:
elliemasters.com/Bookbub
Instagram:
elliemasters.com/Instagram

Final Thoughts

I hope you enjoyed this book as much as I enjoyed writing it. If you enjoyed reading this story, please consider leaving a review on Amazon and Goodreads, and please let other people know. A sentence is all it takes. Friend recommendations are the strongest catalyst for readers' purchase decisions! And I'd love to be able to continue bringing the characters and stories from My-Mind-to-the-Page.

Second, call or e-mail a friend and tell them about this book. If you really want them to read it, gift it to them. If you prefer digital friends, please use the "Recommend" feature of Goodreads to spread the word.

Or visit my blog https://elliemasters.com, where you can find out more about my writing process and personal life.

Come visit The EDGE: Dark Discussions where we'll have a chance to talk about my works, their creation, and maybe what the future has in store for my writing.

Facebook Reader Group: Ellz Bellz

Thank you so much for your support!

Love,
Ellie

Dedication

This book is dedicated to you, my reader. Thank you for spending a few hours of your time with me. I wouldn't be able to write without you to cheer me on. Your wonderful words, your support, and your willingness to join me on this journey is a gift beyond measure.

Whether this is the first book of mine you've read, or if you've been with me since the very beginning, thank you for believing in me as I bring these characters 'from my mind to the page and into your hearts.'

Love,
Ellie

THE END